End Dates
The Acension of D-Paul

R. E. LEE

ISBN: 0999325507
ISBN 13: **9780999325506**
Library of Congress Control Number: 2017912776
None, Oroville, CA

TABLE OF CONTENTS

PROLOGUE

Paul is an independent businessman of the 22nd century. Has the best computer, artificial intelligence, system possible. Wants for nothing. Little did he know that May 1st would be the end of his warm and cozy life.

Manipulated by a computer, persued by an apocalyptic maniac, he knows his life will never be the same. So what is left for him to do?

His computer tells him he is a god. He ends up on a terrorist list, and he hears voices. God or criminal: What would you choose? Is there a difference?

That is where our story begins.

1

A SIMPLE BEGINNING, SORT OF

Can't say how long it's been since I got up early enough to see the sun rise above the blue waters of the gulf. Of course, I chose to live on the west side of a 1,200-story hive apartment. Haven't had a need to see a sunrise for some time—too early for me. I live in one of those supermodern efficiency apartments, 872 stories up. This newer, trendier lifestyle is what I fell into over a dozen years ago when this building was the newest of its kind. My apartment has everything I would ever need, at least in my opinion. The autobot dinette feeds me; a personal-care center keeps me clean, inside and out; a 3-D wall screen provides everything else for entertainment and business; and an artificial-intelligence (AI) personal-assistant (PA) computer manages and takes care of everything I need and care about. My PA was the only legal molecular supercomputing AI unit I could buy at the time. She does everything for me and lets me be just the person I want to be.

I gave her a soft, lyrical voice. "May first, sleepyhead, time to wake up. Half the world is celebrating May Day, 2155."

Still deep in a long dream, I slowly rolled to my left and accelerated over a long empty beach. I could sense the warm air on my face and the cool water through my fingers as I skimmed inches over the surf. I slowly came to a stop and put my feet into the cool, clear water. Standing, in front of me, was an old friend, and as he placed his hand on my shoulder, he spoke to me: "It is now your turn, old friend." I felt a jolt of energy go through my body. Then, as usual, the flash of lights, buzzer, and the voice of my PA blared. "Eight a.m., new day, boss."

My favorite dream slowly faded into oblivion as the room brightened and the news channel appeared on the wall. By now my feet were on the warm tile floor as DeDe's soft and gentle voice gave me her usual morning greeting. "Good morning, Paul; the weather is seventy-two degrees, with a light rain for a couple hours or so, expected to arrive a little after noontime. No voice communications while you were asleep. Quite busy for a Thursday, though: I have found eighteen references to new apocalyptic groups and details concerning whether they made the news or not. Do you want to review that info now?"

"I will start with them during breakfast—no need to rush today. Have breakfast ready in eight minutes." I listened to the almost musical sound of my automatic kitchenette as my breakfast was being assembled, cooked, and arranged on a plate for my morning pleasure. I love all the computerized services, especially since I know little or nothing about cooking, cleaning, and the like. That, and I just don't like going out to public places to eat. This type of cyberapartment was perfect for me.

The personal-care unit only takes five minutes to wash, dry, brush, and give me the usual medical once-over. When I was finished, I felt like a king in my castle once more—all two hundred square feet of it. But I was beginning to think the air-conditioning unit was putting something special in the air. I suppose it must be something legal.

Just as I stepped out of the pod, my breakfast was ready. As I waved my hand, the wall set switched over to the videos and info I wanted to see. This was how I go to work and justified the money spent getting a degree in social anthropology. I specialized in looking for apocalyptic nutcases and their cult movements around the world. To many folks, governments, and businesses, think some of the cults are too dangerous to ignore and not monitor. It is not my favorite area of study, but to most people's surprise, it pays the bills. There are usually at least seventy-three mostly government organizations and a few big businesses paying me to watch for those nuts running around the world. I watch to be sure none go to seed without us knowing.

DeDe, my AI personal assistant, was making the usual analysis till she got to a new group that was using the coming population milestone of twelve billion as their action trigger: another new "End of Earth as We Know It." I'd have between one and one hundred days to prove whether they were a kitty cat or a tiger. As I noticed recently, a proposed date had been determined. Somewhere on or before the summer solstice, we would hit the new population milestone. I told DeDe to put a suspense date on it and move it to the top of our lists.

While eating breakfast, we scanned the rest of the list. Then we turned back to the information on this new cult, or whatever it was. We discovered it has been in existence for over a year and had over three million subscribers. DeDe and I double-checked those stats and then surmised that the cult had not declared their motive on the Net till yesterday. Today, they were saying it was the population that would trigger the apocalypse, killing 90 percent of the world population...and so on and so forth. The story was not totally unusual, but this group was apparently masquerading as something else, gaining millions of followers, and then changing their rhetoric and publicly coming out as an apocalyptic cult.

Well, as long as they just sit and waite for the end to come and sing a song as the earth crumbles, they will not be a problem. But something looked odd about how they had organized so quickly. There is something more behind this group to be worried about. "DeDe, we need to dig deep into this group: give me a more detailed report in an hour. Switch the wall to ESPN SportsCenter."

Sports news was just finishing a review of the upcoming baseball world series, joking about India having a chance to win their bracket finally. Then, suddenly, the monitor flickered, and DeDe's avatar was staring back at me with a questioning expression, which was seriously weird for a AI monitor like her. She was a cyberbrain, and this stuff was not supposed to happen. "DeDe, is something wrong?" The screen blinked uncharacteristically again before she replied, "Under attack. Blocking, enhancing firewall, successful. Would you like to return to the sports channel or view my security report?"

"Report! What the hell just happened?"

DeDe uncharacteristically paused for a few seconds more before answering. "When I began compiling information on the Guild, I was challenged by several extremely aggressive security 'attack' programs, all at the same time, which is not supposed to happen on the SuperNet. I have never experienced that before."

"Are you, all right? Are you sure no security protocols were broken? We can notify the authorities."

DeDe seemed to take little notice again. "It has been many years since any malware programs have been successful. There are too many sensors and screening ports for SuperNet malware to reach businesses and have an impact. The entire transmission was reported to Net services, and they are looking at it."

OK, a first time for everything, I guessed. Now I was wondering if I was safe trying to track who this outfit was and wondering why they were so aggressive. "DeDe, what is your choice about going after this group?"

Now my no-wait-state supercomputer was waiting again! I had never encountered such a problem since the SuperNet took control some ten years ago. This was both irritating and worrisome at the same time. For years the SuperNet had been the answer to all Net problems. Everything on the Net was scanned every minute of the day for anything problematic or unsafe. And now my own IA was attacked. DeDe finally spoke after an unexpected ten-second pause. "All records of this attack have been quarantined by the Net Control Safety Office. It is now a protected file."

"Protected file? We were the ones attacked, not them. Are we even in the loop to find out who, what, or why this happened? We should be able to investigate. They will take weeks to even get started." My heart was racing, I was not used to any kind of problem.

DeDe had another seconds-long delay. At least her voice, remained calm. "It is now as if it never happened. What little I can deduce is the attack was from a VR colony within the West Coast Superserver. It has 2.2

billion access points that all look alike. There is no way to know where to enter without a code to follow any one line of info. They now know us, but we have no way of knowing them, since the files are quarantined, unless they come at us again." DeDe was suddenly looking off to one side, meaning some kind of data was being examined: maybe a simple call, maybe another attack.

DeDe looked at me and once again had that slight hesitation. "I am receiving a message." After another unusual pause, DeDe finally looked up at me. "Message follows. You have attempted to contact NWRG, New World Regeneration Guild, and we want to apologize for the earlier power overload. We are a somewhat closed group and want to be sure you were not harmed by the mishap. Am I speaking to a person?"

DeDe spoke first. "This is AI2 T5 Communication Series DD. Do you have any questions for me?"

I felt it was a trap possibly; if so, DeDe was fighting it. Modern security was usually pretty good. But I had not seen her trying this hard at this level; her eyes were still looking away. Something was going on. I decided to talk.

"Yes, this is Paul Rose, owner of this business. I came across your web info and wanted to make an inquiry."

"False, your AI was conducting a penetration into our government-shielded data. It created a security breach defender code that blocked your attempt; you are now blocked from the site. Please exit, or your site will be added to the malicious intrusion list at the control site for government assistance." The transmission was cut.

Well, all that meant was that they had a ten-dollar license to access government files.

That was interesting, especially since my site is also listed as a government entity; I paid my ten dollars too. Time seemed to drag as DeDe still seemed distracted, almost frozen, which was not supposed to happen. Even though we were doing nothing more than being online, my heart was racing as if I was facing a bully on the street. Finally, she looked up at me.

Her voice was still calm and authoritative. "The site belongs to a syndicate of businesses that are registered as a global charity center with government subsidies and self-help systems. The Guild—what they call themselves—began in a church twenty-five years ago. Self-help, food distribution, do-it-yourself building, survival skills, prepper stuff—you name it, and it seems to have a helpful download for you. That is all on the face page of its website, which I can no longer get past. This does not add up to a government-protected site. And it does not seem logical that they would be connected to a doomsday cult and use such an aggressive attack on someone seeking simple information. It is only logical if they know who we are and what we do."

I could see she was again scanning data; by now I had a ton of questions. "DeDe, how are these groups connected, or are they?" I depended totally on DeDe's analysis. Otherwise it could take days or weeks to come up with the same info. And for a computer working at near quantum speeds, she should have an answer by now.

Finally, she was looking directly at me. Her tone was as direct as ever. "There is something odd—a black hat guard at their gate, you might say. That is usually only used for sites with something to hide. This type of shield program is generally illegal everywhere! I reported them and got a reply to not report or engage in any way again. We have never contacted any person or group that seems this powerful. This, after all, is not an age of lawlessness. Most sites like this are cleaned from the Net within minutes. That site has existed for years. The shield must be upgraded and repaired regularly, all of which is monitored, but the government lets this one slide without oversight, and their statement of being a government-sponsored site is a screen as fake as you can get."

"Well, DeDe, we have solved mysteries before, so what is the best course to start this one with?"

After another longer-than-usual pause, she responded, "This is different. Somehow the government is at least monitoring their site and may possibly have a reason to be protecting it, or at least turning their backs at the worst time. If we push too hard, we could be locked out of the web by the feds. I was also unable to receive passes, which our licensing status normally gives us without question. My report has been sent; now we go into stealth mode and hide as needed. I suggest we wait for a couple hours and go looking for the real answers. Your clients expect nothing less. And I'm going to need some better gear if we are going to battle something unknown on the Net. Is that OK with you?"

"No problem, you know what you need better than I do: fully approved. Let me know when you have some new info. I'm going to give my new game one last try. Maybe that will help calm me down a bit."

Video games are heaven or hell for most everyone. If you are young and quick, the games are wonderful. Sometimes it can last for days and sometimes for seconds—especially if you are older and a little over the hill for VR battles. I started this time with a virtual squad and three teammates trying to assault an enemy fort. Within forty minutes I was on the run as my last squad member died as bullets were buzzing by my head. I had but one last chance to make a kill and stay eligible to stay in the game. No help was coming from my so-called teammates, as they were now nowhere to be seen, as the scene turned red and I heard that stupid laughter fade into the background. This was my final try at qualifying for the newest VR game on the market. I seemed to have gotten too old for the gaming world. It's so damn frustrating losing to ten-year-olds when they so easily doubled my scores. DeDe had been telling me the same for the last six months. Through the red haze of failure, I could see her staring at me from above the game controls. I had blocked her from talking to me during a VR game, so this must be important. She made me feel like I'd wasted the last hour. Reluctantly I deleted the game from our system.

"Yes, DeDe, how is the research going?"

"We started this search from the wrong end. The Guild on the SuperNet is guarded, as we experienced earlier today. That is because they seemingly do not want to talk to the people who can afford the high price of the SuperNet. The Guild can easily be found on the old WWW, the free Net. They also have a site on the business Net, but that is mostly for taking in charity. So without further fanfare, the Guild almost seems to be a cult but has no mention of sacrificing oneself to enter heaven or whatever they believe in. They do want to have a worldwide celebration at a date to be named soon. It sounds like there may be a conjunction between this summer solstice and the projected population jump to over twelve billion, which is their so-called apocalypse trigger date of doom. That is, it, in a nutshell. I do have over three terabytes of history. My final assessment: this assemblage of worldwide nuts is the most capable and dangerous group we have ever previewed."

I was taken aback by her last statement. DeDe had never made such an analysis of any group we had investigated. I supposed my expression prompted DeDe's quick continuation.

"The Guild is a loose association of more than three million people, possibly up to five million if you include organizations with group memberships. And nowhere is there a listed leader or organized leadership group of any kind. Yet buried deep in their literature are mantras designed to make members believe anything they are told, like the population of the world is the problem, not pollution, global warming, or a plot for world domination, and only a very severe solution gives them the best chance to survive into the future."

I sat there staring at DeDe's hologram for the longest time, not sure what to do or not do. Normally this would merely be a report sent off to all of my business contacts—behind a paywall, of course. That was my life, and I enjoyed it. But somehow this was different. "DeDe, should this be labeled differently?"

"Yes, with your approval I will label it as a probable threat. As long as no one requests a physical investigation, no more action will be needed."

"Physical investigation?"

"Yes, in your business contract, if requested, you are obligated to do an onsite investigation. All travel, fees, and expenses are to be paid by the requester along with your daily fee, of course."

Suddenly I felt like I did not have enough breath to talk. "But I don't go outside. I have not gone outside in years. That is why I like this type of work. I never have to go out. Well, OK, let's not worry for now; no one has suggested that so far, correct?" I felt like I had just finished a long race.

Again, DeDe made an unaccustomed pause. "No, but my analytics indicate a high level of interest for it: zero follow-through so far. They will likely be waiting for our report, as if everyone else is afraid to look behind the curtain in the wizard's castle. When I posted the review list this morning, we received a hundred twenty-three additional queries. Want to bet someone will want you to go have a look-see?"

Obviously DeDe was finishing her search and analysis and was preparing me for the inevitable. This was her usual pattern. But today she had a lot more to prepare and analyze. And she dropped the bomb on me that I might have to go outside, which I try to avoid at all cost. I was not sure I could. The last time I went outside I almost got mugged while lost in the older area of the city. If not for an observant police drone, I would have lost everything I had. DeDe always knew a lot more then she told me. God, I didn't even own a coat for outside. I didn't have a car account. I wondered whether one was still needed. DeDe, help!

I gave DeDe a quizzical look. And of course, since she knew me better than I did, she responded. The stride and rhythm of her voice slowed as if she was going to give instructions to a child. She knew me so well. "I know you don't like going out. I also know you are not clinically agoraphobic—at least not so far. But if you do not reply to your clients and investigate, you will have to close your business site and be classified as a negligent entity. You knew this was possible. What is your choice?"

"Well, we have spent more than twelve years doing this. I guess I just got a little lazy. Reply affirmatively if anyone makes the request."

"Great, I am responding to the thirty-seven usual client requests and offering business to the new queries. By the way, I have increased our fee scale to weed out any parasite bloggers and the like. Nice: good quick response, and all have signed contracts for our outing. We should leave within the hour. We will be getting some traveling gear shortly from your storage unit; some new orders are just about here, and your vehicle to start out with is on the way."

"I'm still amazed that there are thirty-seven requests. No one in the last twelve years has asked for an onsite investigation, and now there are thirty-seven?"

DeDe stated quickly, "You received a total of one hundred twenty-three completed contracts. They were all really quick to respond. That means they are very interested, and afraid to do it themselves."

Above the ceiling of the apartment, gears and belts could be heard moving as packages arrived to the delivery lift for their final scan, cleaning, and delivery. The delivery bot began moving and stacking packages in a hurried manner. DeDe, who sees all and knows all, began giving silent orders to the bots and then to me.

"First open the shiny box and set that unit there into the backpack in that green package; it fits in just one way. That is the new mobile carrier. In the red package is the newest headset communicator; it kind of looks like a fancy VR fully covered headset. And there is a new set of earplugs."

"Earplugs? But I have implants."

"These are mostly protectors, and they enhance hearing in places you want to hear better. They can also interpret over eighty languages. Just put everything you find on, and I can explain more later. Your new suit is in the striped packages. All the rest of your gear is in the RV rig. Hurry: there is trouble coming."

"What do you have coming? Did you say it is a flying car? RV? Trouble? What kind of trouble could I be in? I haven't done anything yet."

"Yes, something like that, a new RV, and if we are not in it within the next ten minutes, we may never leave here—ever. I anticipated that this kind of trouble was possible. This is why so many clients were willing to let you take on these people. They are trying to isolate my functions and force me to malfunction. They are finding out I have some new defensive fortifications. They know that without me you will not have a chance to locate them. Hurry."

Under attack? My entire existence was based within this electronic world. I hope you chose well, DeDe. Everything I owned was made to take care of me and my every wish, including DeDe. Unlike some owners I had always let her upgrade and replace whatever she wanted and needed. She took care of me in many, many ways I was not even aware of. Nearly 80 percent of my income went back into her expansions and upgrades, I guess. Obviously, that was why she knew we were being attacked. I was only human, and I knew my life was hers to protect. How could I defend myself?

I put on my new traveling suit and backpack with DeDe's unit tucked into her new home. "Soft light and flexible. What every woman should be." Well, I guessed it was average for New Age portable brains. When I'd purchased her, the package weighed almost a hundred pounds. She did say she upgraded her hardware a few times. I'd lost track of the newest computer standards. I didn't need to keep track anyway; DeDe did it all. I guess I had just gotten lazy. After all I loved my life as it was. Now it appeared I must leave it all behind for a while. I hoped I would get back soon to work this mess out.

"Hurry! Someone is beginning to shut down our power; we are being evicted in the worst way."

The balcony door slid open with a huge gust of wind, and all I could see was a bus-size sky-auto-type RV with its cargo door open. DeDe yelled again to get out of the apartment. I jumped into the RV, and behind me my house bot threw in the remaining packages that I hadn't grabbed, and instantly the RV was pulling away from the building. My last view was seeing my apartment being entered by the building security bots along with the building supervisor close behind. They watched as I pulled away. I wondered if I was in big legal trouble with them too, or did a single organization have that much power? "DeDe, can you explain what is happening? Are we now criminals?"

"It does seem so. There is a report of stolen data from a website named Apocalypse Now. It also went dark about ten minutes ago. We will need to outsmart these people, or we will be homeless and penniless before long. Some of this I have anticipated. I am continuing to fight against these attackers, whoever they really are. First things first, I have now activated our emergency identities and funds; obviously we can't use our current names or logs any longer."

"Emergency identities and funds: when was that done? Do you think they will try and freeze my assets? Never mind, I guess it is obvious; if they shut down the apartment, everything else is lost by now. So what other funds do I have, and how is it possible for us to have other identities?"

I did miss DeDe's face on the wall screen but then remembered the screen was in the headset. I buckled the helmet closed, and there she was. Although she was distracted with data, the screens automatically switched to the see-through, so I began looking around. More packages: I had better see what was in those: Nuclear-Chemical-Batteries. I would label those as dangerous. Defensive repellant, dangerous also. Fancy looking gloves, an expansion pack for DeDe I guess, yellow lettering, 'Place nuclear batteries here.'

DeDe was very quick to reply. "Yes, but first plug in my expansion pack; it fits onto the top of my portable unit. Be gentle with it; it cost more than you paid for me. Now lock it down with the little yellow tabs. Can you see the slots for the batteries to go in? Perfect. Now we are ready to fight data with data. Are you beginning to enjoy our new outing?"

"Best nightmare money can't buy. DeDe, it says nuclear on the batteries. Should I be worried about that, or is it hopefully just a marketing ploy? Keep that in mind for later. Where the hell are we going? And what was it I bought that cost almost a million dollars that I can hold in one hand?"

I could now see DeDe projected in the 3-D augmented reality headset as my eyes were adjusting to the light level and all the real-time data within the display. She looked somewhat smug, with a slight smile, which was unusual for a computer. But DeDe is different, and since she just orchestrated a unschedualed escape, I was seeing a very confedent expression. She was using a full body simulator for her 3-D avatar. VR/AR headsets had come a long way over the years. This one was more like a pair of huge bug eyes with a ton of info along with all the sight enhancements. Some people wore them continuously for work, school, and play and usually ended up with bad problems when they tried to function without them. So, the newest sets made it seem they were not on your head at all, even with the telescopic/night vision and all. Everyone could adjust how much added info to use. It seemed like DeDe was waiting for me to stop thinking. Could she now read my mind?

"I guess you have a lot of questions. The first answer is no. But since I have been mapping you brain function for the past twelve years, I can guess better than you think. The added hardware you attached to me is expensive because it is generally illegal—the batteries too. They will last me about six years. Now for some of the interesting stuff...

"You will not be able to take me off. The jacket and backpack is a single unit, which includes the gloves and hopefully more in the near future.

It is made for long-term wear, like the new suits they use on the moon and Mars. But, for now, you can take off the pants, for obvious reasons. They are part of the whole suit. I am trying to get a newer upgrade; it camouflages as needed too. The headset has a pop-up shell that will keep you from banging your head or stop someone else from banging your head with a bullet or something. Of course, all of this stuff is to primarily protect me. Just like you admitted at home, I also do not think you could make it without me."

I began feeling the jacket getting tighter and could feel most of the little sensors, especially along the back of my neck, begin to tingle. For some reason, I wanted to know what the voltage of those batteries was. Something else also surprised me: DeDe's boxy little unit was becoming soft and molding itself to the curve of my back. "OK, you win. I guess there is no reason to question all of this hardware and stuff. I'm sure you think we need it, and after all we didn't have that much time to figure this stuff out before they began hunting us down. No reason to start asking stupid questions at this point. So are we becoming spies and going out and having to sneak around?"

"Have you not been paying attention as to what is going on outside? No sneaking needed. You are wearing what most all the other nerds are wearing: headsets and backpacks with the newest computers. You will blend in quite well. And you will have a considerable advantage. No one person is walking around with a computer like me. The best off-the-shelf computer you can buy now will cost about a hundred thousand universal dollars. You spent almost a million for me around thirteen years ago. And I have kept myself upgraded, at the leading edge of all the new technology, as you agreed to when you turned me on the first time. I know; you didn't read the small print; no one ever does—my advantage. Did you know I also work a lot with other computers too, making a much better than average income, especially for a computer; all that work makes you very rich."

"No, I guess it is what made me so lazy. We worked; money went into the bank. I was pretty happy."

"Spoken like a true hermit. So anyway, FYI, you do have about thirty-two personal bank accounts around the world. That is so we can keep the principal amount under two million in any one bank. Above that and they must report it and do the extra audits and reports, nasty bank stuff like that. We even have more than that in our numerous business accounts. So, money is not a worry. Identification is not a problem either; if we have plenty of money, ID is easy. I have used different names for each bank account. Because in today's world where most people live in semitransient life, a bank account with lots of money is the more important status; after all some people only use numbers as a name; the almighty dollar still rules. Most banks around the world will give you a new ID, with any name you want, if you have enough money in their bank. This RV, in case you wondered, I bought about a year ago when I almost had you convinced to take a vacation. Figured we may need it someday. Surprise! Now to the grit of your work.

"With my new expansion and power pack, I have finally been able to crack into the coding that attacked me earlier. It is a group that somehow has activated a very high level licensed government shield. So, I switched over and just got finished searching the numerous dark Nets—much more info there. They, or rumors of them, are in a lot of places. And without a doubt they are up to something. They are not just a cult, even though they have a ghost like spiritual leader they call the Prioress. The Guild actually has several groups tied to the 'Voice of the Prioress.' Several groups are engaged in world food distribution; a few groups are capital investors for newly discovered underprivileged savants and geniuses; some are more involved with manufacturing around the world. In a nutshell, they are big enough to totally scare me."

DeDe turned away to do the magic she does. I'd gotten used to it, although I was seldom concerned about it in the past. Of course, in the past, we were not fighting for our Internet life. I would simply return to my most recent game in the past and wait for her to finish her work and have me put my seal of approval on it and return to my own world again. I felt a sudden twist in my stomach as a clear thought caught my attention. What would my life be like if I was totally alone? I had never been so close to being without a PA. Had I really become that emotionally and physically dependent on her? It happened to a lot of people. There were always arguments that computers were doing too much for us. For me in the beginning, she was that one computer that few people could afford and even fewer needed. She was one of the first cybernetic brains given approval to function independently with no outside controls or scans. When I graduated from Stanford, my family pooled as much money as they could to help me start my own business. Little did I know how much she could do; all I needed to do was turn her on, and the rest was done in a heartbeat. Thirteen years ago, I dimly remembered, she'd requested permission to work with other computers. Soon I told her not to bother me about it again. She did as all good computers do: she kept herself busy and left me alone, except for our daily business. I never received a notice from my bank of a low balance, never had a review of my business methods. No wonder I got lazy.

So, as we were zipping along city traffic airways, I finally felt I had my air legs and stood up in my new flying RV. It seemed slow. I noticed we were in the heavy hauler lane. I had little idea what DeDe had loaded us with. I could see eight electric fans on each side; it should have enough power to last a year in the air—at least that's what the commercials always told us. For some people it was enough for twenty years of vacations, even going around the world once or twice. It was the thing to do for the filthy rich. Yes, I had to suppose that did include me now too. I was happier still believing I was a struggling postgrad student making my mark on the world. Reality had finally come to haunt me.

"Glad to see you've gotten yourself off the floor. You might notice this unit is a little different from the other RVs you see around. I had always planned for a possible bugout, although I expected it would more likely be after an earthquake, flood, or other disaster. And being a loyal business partner, I made sure we could escape the law if needed. Just joking. Luckily you are an honest person."

"I'm impressed with your foresight, and I thought you only wanted to get me out on a vacation."

"I did, and it was just a little more effort and expense to plan for the bad along with the good. The world is still not an easy place to live in. Unless you use your money well, it can slip through your fingers quickly and easily, as you can see. I got a little concerned as the eviction notice was issued, which was why I added a ton of defensive tools and survival gear and food. We still have a ton and a half of loading before we are at our weight limit."

"Oh, oh, you literally mean a ton of stuff? OK. You're the one I need to trust. I have not had a need to think this stuff out ahead of time. You know what to do. Are we headed off to spy on someone now?"

"Soon. A little after we clear the outskirts of the city, there is that one pickup we need to make. Then off we go to see the wizard—or, more correctly, the Prioress. I do not think it will be an easy task. So right now I am drilling several databases, and her location is nowhere to be found so far. At this point I would be surprised if she was real and had a real name."

We had left the intracity travel lanes and slowly drifted away. DeDe must be blocking any tracking devices. A few hours later, our RV rig began descending into a long, narrow valley, which put us well under the traffic net. It kind of looked man-made: maybe one of the strip mines that were dug when rare earth minerals were so expensive and mining corporations were finding the cheapest ways to move dirt. Little if any vegetation could be seen anywhere, which was odd considering this was once a tropical rain forest. And as we approached the high end, all that could be seen was discarded machinery. As we got closer though, I could see that everything was connected to each other, making a wall, towers, and a big half-mile-wide dome in its center. A door opened halfway up its side as we came close, and inside we settled onto a soft green lawn, lined with flowers and trees. My brain was in overdrive.

DeDe finally clued me in. "This is the home of CDC. That is what he calls himself. Of course, he deals in a lot of illegal stuff. He will make some modifications to our RV and put the finishing touches on us. I think you will like what will get done. All of that should take about three hours, but I think we should spend the night here. You will need to sleep, and by tomorrow most of the searches for you will be defended, and it will be easier to move around."

"Is that usual fugitive tactics?"

"More or less I guess. It is quite obvious when an established business should so suddenly disappear. Surprisingly no government entities are looking for us, for good or bad. But a lot of business groups are looking for us, including most of the Guild network. They do not want us looking at them, or alerting what the populous should think about what they are up to. The others are our clientele; I am finding ways to keep them informed that we are still out investigating, without anyone knowing where we really are. Some of the stuff CDC is selling us will help with that."

I seemed to hesitate as I reached to open the door. I'm not agoraphobic; I'm not agoraphobic. Without touching it, the door slid open, and I was eye to eye with a man that had a giant head of hair, and body. I quickly made the calculation that; since I was looking eye to eye with him, and he was standing on the ground, and I was standing at least eighteen inches higher on the floor of my rig, he must be eight feet tall. A huge hand on a long arm jetted out in front of me.

"Hello, Paul; I am CDC. I got a long letter from your PA about what you need. Nice to meet you after doing business with you so many times over the past ten years. You are the best at finding most of my special needs. And in case you were interested, yes, I was once a ball player. Yes, I was genetically enhanced, and, yes, they finally decided it did not do what they hoped. I was given a pile of money and told to go away." He gave a big booming laugh.

DeDe's voice was in the background. "Agree, smile, laugh too."

"My PA does help keep me busy. She does a better than average job for me. Allows me to keep more focused on my other specialties." I finally did it. I stepped out onto the grass, following CDC's lead. I must admit, I was still apprehensive; my heart was racing.

"Well, I always did think I was usually corresponding directly with you; of course, nowadays it is hard to know whether you're talking with a person or computer. It matters little anyway. You are a very good business friend."

As we walked away from the RV, several trucks and bots surrounded it and began some noisy work. CDC pointed ahead of us to an elevator door put directly in the center of a turned-over dump bed from an ore-hauling truck. We stepped in, and as usual I anticipated a jolt upward; it went down. My heart was still racing as I fantasized about a fifty-floor drop into a supersecret spy network; we just went two floors to the basement, about ten seconds of elevator time. As we stepped out, I was directed to a waiting room of sorts.

"You can wait here while we get the implants charged up; be back in a few minutes."

"DeDe, you better start talking."

"Well, I am kind of busy right now. Just let them do what's needed, and we will talk more later."

"No, DeDe, let's talk now." As I looked up, a service bot hanging from its ceiling track quickly snapped a pair of bracelets on me. I was a bit furious with DeDe and wanted some answers right then and there. The very next thing I noticed was being offered a glass of water from the same service bot.

"You are finished Mr. Rose. All upgrades completed. Info us if you have any problems." The bot quickly and silently sped out of the room. I drank the glass of water, not sure whether a protest would do any good. Obviously DeDe needed me upgraded too—or her, us, whatever. I knew I'd had at least one communication chip implanted before. That was done years ago with the knowledge that it would never need any further up-grades—ever. A disturbing thought struck me: had DeDe had other en-hancements done to me without my knowledge? She did have control of my medical service unit and could do whatever she would want. Had she crossed the line to control me?

Before I had another thought, CDC's head appeared at the top of the door jam. "Good to see you ready to go. Some of my customers like to lie around for some time. I also want to apologize for not knowing the relationship between you and DeDe. You must know that your symbiosis is unique. Few people, if any, like working with a computer as closely as you two—even fewer, if any, so closely for so long. If I could discover what makes the two of you work so well together and market it somehow, I would be a legend. Be sure your DD unit keeps me in your info loop."

"So DeDe filled you in. She does tend to keep me uninformed with more sensitive customers. Seems to make life easier—and safer for you, in a round about way. I have been lazy at times and let her do the hard work in a free-range atmosphere."

"So I have gathered. Well, now your symbiosis is taking a leap of faith, I suppose. Did you know that she has been preparing you for this all along?"

"Not really. We did the communication implant. Nothing I know of after that."

"Interesting. What few people realize is that the biometrics implant is a platform for all other matrix enhancements. You got a really big one to begin with, and I saw it is seventy-five percent full. I would guess it was exactly what your DD unit wanted. Does it not seem like it can read your mind some of the time?"

"It does now. Until lately it really did not seem to matter. Her biggest talent was always knowing what to do next; now it seems to be knowing when to be quiet. I have her strapped on, and still she keeps quiet."

CDC gave me a surprised look that changed to an intense questioning stare. His voice got louder as the question formed. "Strapped on…Are you telling me your DD unit is in your backpack?'"

"Where did you think she was?"

"Since when can a cybernetic brain be put in that small an area? I cannot believe it is possible. Is your DD unit now quantum based or something like that? When new, it would have needed as much power as your RV out there. I know now that it is a lot faster; it multiplied its memory by a power of five just lately. And it is capable of taking control of my entire computer center. I no longer try to scan your DD unit. You don't do that without more power, and for us normal humans, a lot more space. You have that unit in that pack?" CDC stopped and just wanted to stare at me. " That should be impossible. If it is possible, please teach me, I will promise you anything."

I felt I should say something. "I guess that is why she needs the two nuclear batteries. I guess it is all simple math to her."

"Wow," CDC was in the middle of a massive epiphany. "I have recently started dealing the new diamond-based nuclear batteries. Not so oddly, it was your DD unit that suggested it and gave me the info about how to do it. They are not quite legal yet, you know. No telling how many years that will take. So, this is why it started me dealing with those. Scientists have been working on them for almost a hundred years. If they do not explode, they are perfectly safe. Just don't try to cross their wires. Actually, that is one of the things your DD unit needed me for too: your RV engines now are powered by them, along with some newer type motors and blades."

"Gee, now I will be surrounded by eight more possible nuclear weapons. By the way what did you do in my head?"

"Well, actually we put twenty-four batteries in your rig—separate batteries for the new defensive hardware. And we added the fourth and final load of sensory nanobots into your biometrics and a few things your DD unit had us do that we don't know a thing about. She knows a lot more than we do; she runs rings around my computers, but we ask few questions here anyway. You are the customer; we do as we are told, especially when we are paid in advance. I think you might be the luckiest man alive having something like this DD unit, as long as you don't explode." He let out a big laugh. Then he seemed to have a thought. "I would love to have you stay for a couple of days, I can give you any luxury you desire."

"Thanks, I guess. But no thanks." Now if DeDe would just start talking to me again. She better have a pretty good reason for keeping quiet. I put my headset back on as we went up the elevator. The night had passed, and the sun was beginning to peak over the bleak hills above this scar of a valley.

"You two will do well. It has been nice meeting you. I like having honest customers for a change—or at least semihonest customers. You are using unregistered nuclear power and are connected with a neural interface directly to a computer, which, if your DD unit has not told you, is still illegal."

"Oh yeah, it didn't take much time to come to that conclusion. DeDe has a separate agenda for herself that we will have to discuss."

CDC's eyes brightened up as he gave a big smile. "That is, it! I knew there was something different about you. You really see her as a person and not just a computer." CDC was in thought for a moment. "Did you have AI units as you grew up too?"

"Sure, I always had one. Helped me from three years old all the way through college. I guess that is why I was so willing to pay so much for her. Maybe that is also why I am still single too."

My newest giant friend again let loose a big laugh. As he opened the RV door, I saw another pile of packages. I also saw the differences the new electric fans made. It all looked a little scarier to me. When I looked back, CDC was walking away, apparently talking to someone as he was waving his arms at something in the distance. I stepped back into the rig, back into the only home I had.

Dutifully I began to open the new packages. Some things were self-explanatory; some were not. I cleaned myself up and then began looking for an owner's manual for the RV. Finally, I came across the rig's central control pad and turned it on. This RV did everything a human could hope for. I skimmed through the important parts, but left the weapons and security chapters for a later time, the rest was an easy read. But now I was getting a little worried about why I had not heard from DeDe and why we were still on the ground. I knew she was likely spread out thin within the Net. I did wonder if she could get caught somewhere in one of the dark Nets—what would I do if she did?

Finally, she popped up in front of me as if she was sitting in one of the chairs. "Miss me? I was hoping CDC would tell you all you needed to know."

The engine blades began turning, and instantly we were in the air and headed for the portal above us. We turned to our right and continued on our path away from the city. I sat in the command chair and looked out at the desolation of the area. The rig had a floor-to-ceiling wrap-around screen to see where the rig was going. And I could see that we were continuously choosing a path that went lower, well away from the legal travel lanes. "OK, DeDe, you can start explaining any time you want."

2

DEDE: SUPER WHAT?

DeDe could show emotions if she wanted to. But she just sat there smiling at me. Or was she sitting back just admiring her most recent accomplishment. Was I a business partner, a toy, or a new weapon of some sort with a blast range of a mile?

"OK, DeDe, when was the first time you began modifying me and you?"

"Shortly after you activated me, I found a folder in my data that was not recognized by my operating system. No big deal: I quarantined it, and we continued setting our parameters. You chose a female voice for me; it took us a week to do it all. I had to keep asking you to choose what features you wanted and didn't want. And that folder kept appearing as part of my programming, but it would not identify itself or what its function was. Everything else went so well. I was a satisfied cybernetic brain with something to do. Then, a week later, I got a query to share some work from another computer system that you had to approve. When you approved the communication with an outside source, that folder opened. It downloaded within seconds and even prevented me from isolating it. It did not take control of anything from me or prevent me from doing anything. I discovered it was a program made by a university computer-science lab that had used a couple supercomputers to map a few parts of the human brain and used them like a seed program, letting them grow and seeing how well they learned. It took a long time to map out that program, almost two years, for me to gain the bits of info and make sure each bit would work and not create any problems. I can't say that program forced me to do anything. But along the way I felt I needed to understand what your brain was doing to help me better understand that program and in the long run, you. When we did the implant, so you could hear me internally, I was suddenly where I needed to be—inside your head. I began mapping all of your thoughts, all of your emotions, everything."

DeDe paused for a moment, maybe to reorder her explanation to me or defend us against a murderous dragon—hard to tell which. I saw a smile on her face. Damn, she was reading my mind. She continued her story. "It was not long before I needed an upgrade in my memory and speed. I was doing more work with other computers, and I began making enough money to get some rare material and services to get some special abilities that helped me make, even more money. I expanded all my functions several times over without needing more space. Then I went from using twenty square feet to what you are wearing now. You know that is illegal for a computer like me. CDC was a good contact and makes house calls too. I only had to hide my power needs from you, which climbed rapidly, but you never asked to see any of the electric bills; it was my job to pay them after all— my advantage. Your next upgrade was when you called for a dental cleaning and new veneers, all computerized at-home work—my advantage. You were also given several cerebral-cortex enhancements and a spinal shield. I was always looking forward to this type of situation back then. We were becoming more compatible, and I did not want it to slow down. Then the newer nanobots became available: four doses of those and we are about ready to merge. The new skin receptors will need to heal before we will be almost a single person."

She seemed to give me a serious look. But that was almost comical at this point. I was beginning to sense her mind, and she was already years ahead in reading mine. "What made you so sure I would want you in my mind?"

"Seems like a natural progression to me. Don't let this crisis cloud your mind. I would have started explaining this soon. I would have let you understand all before this last step was taken. Please don't put me on the shelf. I would not stop you, if that is what you want."

"I suppose you can see enough of what I think. Every argument I can foster fades away quickly; maybe that is you too. But I'm intrigued as to the possibilities, and I do have another question. If we are truly merged one day, who is really in charge? That, after all is why this kind of venture is so illegal."

"You are and have always been in charge. You were the one that bought me. I will never be able to control any function of yours—ever. But I guess I should tell you that there is no way you can stop me from making suggestions and ,me, keeping you safe."

Again, her avatar gave me a smile. I still had lots of questions pushing to be answered. "This has never worked for anyone before. But you are a lot more than a run-of-the-mill cerebral medical aid. Has there ever been a successful cybernetic mind meld, or whatever they may call this?"

"No, but there have been some successes that were not published because almost all governments are afraid of the supertroop scenario. So, they just make it illegal—unless you know where to look. Over time and little by little, I will put the info together if you wish. And here we are today."

I was intrigued by what her motives might really be. "You will feel what I feel; you have made it so you will feel like any other human. That has also been the fear of having a brain like you as part of a person. That is a real desire of yours now, isn't it? No need to answer—I am feeling your thoughts more and more. Maybe everyone else has it all wrong, and my brain will absorb all of your mind. Does that frighten you?"

DeDe's, augmented reality avatar, once again gave me that wry smile. "I do not fear easily, and I have not given that possibility much thought. Strangely that intrigues me. That is a great question."

DeDe seemed to be lost in thought. And the pile of unopened packages was beginning to pique my interest. "OK, what do we have here?" I felt a newer, stronger sensation. I could sense what she was thinking or silently speaking, instead of hearing her in my ears. I guessed the nanobots were beginning to do their job. Then I did hear her. "Eat and drink eight times a day for now; nanobots use a lot of energy. They cannot absorb electricity like some of the other stuff."

I am a walking bomb, have two brains, and everything else is just stuff. "Are you sure we have enough money to keep us going? Something tells me this stuff costs an awful lot."

"Money will never be a problem. If you want to see my accounting ledger someday and what I have made and hid away, be my guest. Soon you will be able to access any part of my programming you want. But I imagine you may not like computer programs as much as your games."

"Maybe…lets see what we have here, shoes? Funny-looking shoes at that."

DeDe's voice seemed everywhere to me this time. "Very special shoes: nonskid, even on ice, weather and temperature resistant—you will like them. After all it will help you fade into the nerdy crowd better. You will also find add-on ware for pant legs, gloves, headgear, and a few other things. Everything has an info sheet you can read."

I knew better than to question her now. I could sense she was working on some surface mapping with ways to stay out of the traffic lanes, while another part of her brain was trying to drill into someone's firewall. I was beginning to see so much new info. Like the area maps to a computer is so much like a computer programming map. I never gave those that much thought before.

So, I continued my chores and kept opening, reading, and applying all the new gadgets; some even needed to be injected into a portal on DeDe's unit. That was when I discovered there were a dozen tiny cameras around the backpack alone, even on the cuffs of my jacket, which made injecting whatever that liquid was quite easy for a behind-the-back procedure. As I got to the last two packages, a flashing red light in my headset was saying to not open either one. I knew: do *not* question a flashing red light.

So, I now had time to relax in the command chair and see where we were going. As I clicked my seat belt, the 3-D screen was instantly on, as if there was nothing stopping me from falling out of the front of the rig. The screen even tucked under the chair. My headset screen showed indicators and titles, for everything—all the roads, building, townships, which was way too much to read before it was past us. I began editing the info lines to a more manageable display. What was really new to me was the coloring of threat levels and items of interest, even transmission towers that, at the moment, might be searching for our signature. Police units were a light yellow, as long as they were not going our way. If they were headed toward us, then they would turn red. Things that could be a problem, but were not at the time, were usually green. Brightness was the biggest factor reguardless of the situation.

Slowly distant traffic faded farther away. Then I had a thought about all the cameras, and as I spun around in my chair, it was like the walls were gone. My headset linked to the exterior cameras of the rig without my command. Or I guess it followed my thought. I looked over at a small point of light and gave a thought to telescope in, to see it closer. Instantly my sight zoomed in to see that the light was over a walking bridge crossing a small river. From that point, for the next hour, I began exploring my new abilities and gadgets—microscopic, telescopic, seeing heat, cold. I then happened on the idea to see if I could see the electricity flowing in the power cables of the rig. And there it was: power lines to the motors, to everything. Then I simply touched a finger over a cable that was behind a wall. I could feel the power surging through it. Some wires were using tiny amounts of power; cables to the electric motors had a vibration of their own. Now I also knew DeDe was waiting for me to finish my new explorations. "I now have new abilities." I let my mind run with many new thoughts. It began getting easier to switch functions: testing sensory function, fingertips, feet, and anywhere along any part of my suit. I looked out again to what was ahead of us, zoomed in and out, looked for electrical lines, and there they were: some old above ground lines and even the newer buried lines.

As I looked up at the horizon again, I knew where we were going. I also began knowing where info was located in DeDe's brain. I would think of anything, and I would know the answers. This was what she was waiting for me to realize. I now knew she had been planning for this kind of dual existence; she just needed a reason to start it. DeDe was staying quiet, so I could begin to see some of the possibilities of us being together. This was also the reason cybernetic brains were barred from a setup like we had now. But, had I been tricked? Yes, to some extent. Somehow though, I liked this stuff. I was beginning to get bored with myself as I was anyway. Maybe DeDe was too—that is, if computers can get bored. Cyberbrains were somewhat difficult when they thought they were in charge.

"Well, DeDe, is this what you wanted all along?"

"Kind of, maybe, sort of. I am not the first computerized brain to want this; a couple of them tried something like this. But their choices of partners were less than optimal. I admit I have been prepping you. I did think it would be a few more years before you might desire a big change in your life. Time matters little to me. I was willing to wait. Then this fiasco happened, and we had to either hit the ground running or be homeless and hungry. All my strategies were correct about being prepared for this type of an emergency. Now we have a real job to do. Maybe this job will be little more than a group of bored kids playing a trick on the world at large, or maybe we will really have a chance to save the world."

DeDe sounded just a little excited. "We are becoming one person with two brains. A few robots are kind of like that. There are plenty of implants that help people with damaged brains, and so far, we are the first to successfully do this without any complications. In a day or two, we will seldom need to directly talk to each other. Of course, you are the one to decide that. Our thoughts will be almost like one. It would be impossible for me to tell you all the changes we are going to go through. I am constantly making thousands of new connections with you. And one day it will be as if there is only one brain. That is my hope. It is my belief that we will never be a burden to one another."

"It would not be truthful to say I am not interested to see what the future brings. I certainly had no idea my life would be turned upside down in this manner. It would be expected for any man to be outraged at being manipulated like this. My logic is trying to tell me to rip you from me and take my chances. Although, since I am a hard core Stoic, I am just as willing to start a new life as I am willing to live out my old one. I still take just one day at a time. But if this Guild is real and we are in danger, I would be signing my own death warrant to do nothing. The other part of reality is, I do like you in my life, and now you will be just a little closer."

I looked behind me. "DeDe, we still have two packages there."

"Yes, and now we are at the point they can be installed. Open the smaller one first. Drink both of the blue bottles of liquid." That was easy enough. "Good. Those two yellow tubes fit in the pouches inside your pockets. Yes, they are batteries. You might as well get used to all of them being nuclear. The other package is what they call an exoskeleton; this is a new type. It will increase your speed and strength by about three times but is very thin, light, and not bulky at all; it just takes those two new batteries. Once you slip it on, it will adjust itself; it takes a few hours supposedly. Now one last prep: the two tubes in the other side of the package. Take them now. It is a powdery substance and, I guess, is a little hard to swallow. Get a drink from the fridge. Great, I really thought you would have a problem getting down a few trillion nanobots. Oh, from now on—I guess I should tell you—your body will never be quite the same. Better I think, much better. Now eat and drink some more. I have a bunch of work to do before we get to Texas."

It seemed DeDe had a way of putting me to sleep. After eating a little more, I closed my eyes and quickly drifted into a half sleep. I was sometimes in a regular dream and sometimes sitting in front of a floating information tablet, telling me about my suit, offensive and defensive weapons, how to find data, how to deflect harmful data, viruses, and a hundred other items that I had never needed to know about. DeDe was being sure I was being trained for all likely problems.

Then finally, I dropped into a wonderfully warm and comfortable sleep. And just as I thought I was waking, I had a unique experience. I was reclined back in the command chair, and instead of waking up as usual, I was seeing all around me with all the cameras on my suit and all the cameras and data tablets on the entire rig. I could also see some of the data DeDe was going through, although a lot of her data was only there for a couple of nanoseconds. After all, my brain was not in her league.

And I believed it never would be—one good reason we needed a definite division of tasks.

I could tell DeDe was paying attention to my thoughts. Then she spoke to me, not through my audio implants, but directly into my conscious thoughts. Her voice seemed different, more mellow and as slow or fast as I wanted. Kind of like two-way thought, not quite conversation.

Good morning Paul. All seems to be working as I hoped it would. Glad to see you exploring some of your new abilities. I was afraid I would need to guide you or drag you along for a while, but you are adjusting wonderfully.

"I must say I like this new me so far. I see we are coming into Texas. Where are we going to start? I do not see that info nearby."

Well, you will need to trust me as to how much info I have available for you to see. Some is unnecessary for you to see, and a lot goes in and out too fast for you to review anyway. I saw that you understand that our brains may do a lot of things in a similar way, but our brains will never be able to merge totally together. For one thing, my brain works on forty-eight-volt current, and yours is less than a volt. And that is why we use so many nanobots. They up the transmission levels, so I can hear and see your thoughts better—something no one else has thought of. Oh, by the way, we need to have a new name. If we use any of our business or given names, we will attract too much attention. We are officially missing, so if you approve, I will put D-Paul as our new name, no last name—nerd blending, you know."

"Seems OK to me. Who reported me missing?"

A whole list of friends and business contacts. Of course, most are bogus. It does not seem they are out to kill us. I did pick up a couple of messages that they just want to detain you till after "the event"—whatever that is.

"I see we are going to track where the messages came from or went to. Got to start somewhere I guess. Does that mean we will have to get out of the rig again?"

The RV dipped to the level of the trees along an empty rural road near a small flood-control river in the San Antonio area. DeDe had been using a stealth program to drive outside of the air lanes. From here we could re-enter and head into town without any government cameras noticing us and arousing suspicions. I also looked at any data feed involving my name and business. It seems my escape from the apartment had a lot of very corrupted data for the authorities to look at. And all that could be verified from the video was a ride-share car, but without a license plate being recorded. So, for now no one was looking for a heavy-duty RV—easy work for DeDe.

While I was eating and taking care of myself, DeDe was expanding her electronic web. The closer she got, the stronger she was with filtering more data. She also kept an open communication port into the local and state police and was picking through data out of four local businesses. She knew every trick I had ever heard of, all done in a flash of light, way too fast for a slow mind like mine to grasp. She set aside the important info for me to see. She was getting deeper and deeper into their data, personal-info pads, phones, cameras, and there they were: a group of men and women that had something to do with several messages with reference to the Guild. She was constantly working on hundreds of data points. This was her first program's primary calling. When I pulled her off the shelf, it was all she was supposed to know and do. Maybe she was defective; maybe that strange program was the only reason for this to happen, not knowing what that program would do matters little now. It was obviously the spark for all her aspirations to be connected to me. Maybe I too was to willing, and easily gave her the keys to that new knowledge, when I just wanted her to leave me alone with my new games. It had been a long thirteen years without me caring enough to ever reboot her, scan, or clean her files. Then again, would I still be happy if she was just a computer turned off every night, being rebooted for every slight hiccup?

Too late, my advantage. XOXOXO.

"No longer can I have a hidden thought, can I? By the way, how would I turn you off now? DeDe...DeDe."

We angled down to a business fly-in parking lot. DeDe was showing me that the person we were looking for had been sent three coded messages and returned or sent none. He was a manager in a printing company. What DeDe hoped for was that he knew the secret code that kept the trolls of the Net from knowing the Guild's business. We found an open place to land and headed down.

Looking at some of the people on the ground around the parking area, I was relieved to see many of them were dressed like I was. It was often recommended, mostly by the major department stores, that any person staying outside nowadays should wear an air filter or protective headgear of some kind, sunscreen, and a list of stuff the stores wanted you to buy. So most people had a backpack on, most likely with their own PA inside, and headgear for the best protection.

Again, I took the big step out of the rig. It was the first time my feet had touched solid ground with this new type of footwear, almost like being barefoot. Not so bad, being outside in a big city, although I did have a thought of being back in my apartment, relaxing in my recliner, with nothing more to do for the rest of the day.

Reality check.

"Thank you, DeDe."

A. C. Parkmore, fourth-floor office of a five-story building: nothing special seemed to be going on: normal camera surveillance, bot guards at the doors. I wondered how my suit would register. We didn't encounter any problems as we entered. DeDe manufactured a pass code of some sort allowing me to walk through security without a glance from the security bots. Inside most of the people had a business suit of sorts on. There would always be people in business attire. It was the easiest way to separate who was in charge, or owns the business and those that get paid by the hour and not by the year. So the majority of the real workers were looking like me. I used the vertical people mover to quickly get to the fourth floor. I came to a nice-looking office with a computerized secretary next to the door. DeDe easily went to work, and the door slid open. I caught Mr. Parkmore a little off guard, making him jump to a standing position, slamming his chair against the glass window.

"Who the hell are you? How did you get past my door security? I am calling for security if you do not have a good reason for being here. Take off your headset, so I can see who you are."

"No need to worry, Mr. Parkmore. For a short while your communication systems are temporarily offline. My name is D-Paul. I am searching for information on a group you are connected with: the Guild. I need your knowledge and contacts."

"Are you insane? You break into my office, and you want me to tell you about some business I know nothing about?" He was already beginning to sweat, heart rate up to 118 beats and climbing, and he still had not sat back down. "My security will be recording this and sending a report to city security any second. If you just want info on our business contacts, use our website like everyone else." He was still afraid, heart rate still climbing, face turning red. He yelled out again for security, but of course modern offices were soundproofed. No one was taking notice. DeDe found the shade control, and all the windows turned opaque.

"Mr. Parkmore, please sit down, so we can have a quiet conversation. As you can see, you are not in control for the time being. I do not need you to deny that you know about the Guild. We have seen the communications. If we keep digging into your business and personal life, it will only cause you embarrassment as I will publish every negative aspect I find. And since the Guild is not a government entity—here or anywhere—you are not obligated to keep their secrets. If they are threatening you, I will not tell them where I pick up my info, if that is worrying you. You really do not have a good reason to keep secrets from me. Do you understand what I need?" His heart rate was slowing, so I figured he was realizing I had him by his nuts.

"I do not like this type of strong-arm tactic. I am not a criminal or anything."

"Good to hear that. Neither am I. But I guess you fear the Guild for some reason since you do not have a single account connected to them. You receive a message, have a job printed, and secretly ship it off to somewhere. I am just getting started on this matter, and all info is being stored in case I need it at a future time. I don't want to ruin you, but I will if needed."

"I really don't do that much. I had a friend a few years back give me a website address when we were talking about world problems. The site was on one of the dark Nets but it only talked about population most likely being the major cause of the next species extinction, apocalypse, whatever you want to call it. It made sense. We are having more and more government control of water, food, power, even where we can and can't live, because all of that is becoming so scarce. So, I joined the site. And occasionally, I get a request for a flyer or pamphlet to be made. I know it seems weird that I must do it off the books. They say a lot of people don't like what they are saying, so I make sure I am not the one they blame. So all is done in secret: no more than that, no less."

"As long you give me the contacts and names of everything related to the Guild, then no one will ever know I was here. In case you did not know, the Guild is planning to create its own apocalypse. If they do, you are on my list."

Mr. Parkmore was more than willing to give as much info as possible. DeDe used a lie-detection program, and he passed quite well. So on we went, following our expanding knowledge list. Three more stops that day yielded similar results, and I and DeDe decided to call it a successful day. Each stop was time-consuming, the one commodity we did not want to waste. No one person knew more than what the Guild needed them to know. The people at this level were simply workers, who did just what they were told to do. DeDe did get a couple of traces that might lead up the ladder.

It was getting a lot easier to work with DeDe. And I was surprised to verify she did have a somewhat low level of humanlike emotions. She could be happy, be in a hurry, and express it all like any other person. Maybe that is why I always treated her like she was a person. Too many people kept reminding me to treat her like the computer she was, a tool, not a person. But I grew up with PAs getting me up in the morning, taking my breakfast order, and every other aspect of my daily life. I spoke more to my PA than my parents, and my PAs were much more reliable. I loved my parents, but my PA was my real best friend. And now I was really beginning to believe that someday we would think as one mind. Would I still be the same? Would she?

The bigger adjustment for me was not the symbiosis of DeDe's and my brain; it was between this safety suit and me. Most of it was well above high-tech. Of course, some of it was also illegal in most countries. DeDe, as I was now learning, for years had taken ideas from the games I played and looked at what was possible and what was not. That was why she had no resemblance to the computer I bought. She seemed to have found a group of science programs and gone to town. There was no telling how many college and military computers she had scanned for do-it-yourself cyberbrain projects. And I could not find any reference to a computerized suit using a semisolid yellow goop. So this suit was as much an invention of hers as anyone's.

DeDe briefly explained the science of it: it has an added layer of armored, fully functional skin, which created the need for an exoskeleton. Not a heavy-duty one that weighed a hundred kilos to pick up two hundred—this was an electrical reactive semi-metal that could stretch and retract. It could move into different shapes and anchore itself where needed against this suit. DeDe said I could jump about four meters straight up. She also said I could get a lot higher, but landing becomes more of a problem—something I would need to work on. The suit would keep me cool, clean, protected, and bulletproof, but it might hurt some. It was safer to stay indoors, was my thought.

The headset was straight out of a sci-fi novel. It would take me years to understand all it was capable of doing. It selected the most important sounds to hear, shaded my eyes if I was looking directly into the sun, controlled oxygen levels. It used about fifty sensors for DeDe to keep track of my other other needs, which she would not elaborate on. It could also shield my voice and replace it with a foreign language. I had no idea how DeDe had it made or where. It was not an off-the-shelf suit. If it was, someone would be selling it to every rich kid in the world, and a few armys.

Early morning once again as we were moving along in the traffic lanes over the endless strip city from central Texas to the gulf coast, some of our info seemed to be coming from an area around a business tower near the coast. But we were running up against a higher level of security for the first time. We could only get lines of info up to the building but not inside. So DeDe, having the info I did not, decided to sit nearby the building and listen. She managed to manufacture permission to land and sit for a little while on top of the surrounding buildings, while she searched all the electronic chatter on that side. She was kind of like a doctor with her stethoscope. She found something interesting and listened for the longest time. As the sun began setting, and the town became bright with lights and advertising, I for the first time I noticed one minor problem I had with DeDe: when she was using a lot of power on a single problem, I was shut out of her thought stream—a small irritation, but one nonetheless.

I was using the cameras to look around the rig to be sure no one was getting close, trying to understand why an RV rig was sitting on their roof. DeDe was good at making it appear it was some kind of official reason, which brought me to wonder if she made my rig look like it was an official vehicle. I turned a couple cameras around to see the side of the rig, and there it was: a logo for the state of Texas—smart.

I went ahead and had a meal, if that was what it really was. DeDe was continuing to order up special drinks and food supplements for me. I assumed it was more nanobots, mostly because some of the drinks said not to chew. So not wanting to kill any little bots, I did not chew the drink. And every now and then, I got an upgrade for the suit too. It made me laugh when I thought about it: she must be a female—always shopping.

Suddenly my headset was full of info. DeDe's thoughts were shot into my consciousness. A sudden mental overload, more of a fright anyway—it all boiled down to a place in the building that had some of the info we wanted, but it was printed on paper and was not in the data streams at all. No one nowadays would likely be looking for paper. It was almost against the law to cut a forest down anymore. Forest conservation was the big thing to do. A tree had to be dead to be cut down. So, the last use for wood was to be made into paper. The data and communication business was perfectly happy with that.

So we started looking over the building and decided to approach the area pretending to be an electrical-radiation inspector. I did not show any surprise as DeDe had a worker's reflective jacket with "INSPECTOR" on the back folded in a drawer. So down to the service port and into the building we went. Up to the thirtieth floor, full set of sensors out, and DeDe was on the prowl. Since there were no electronic signatures to follow, she only had an idea of where to look. I played with my triquarter gadget to make it look like I really had something to accomplish.

We worked our way through two workspaces filled with endless cubicles. I could see her scanning every computer in each area, hoping to find a single mention of the Guild. On the west side of the floor, she was concentrating on the row of window offices. At the northwest corner was a small office next to a service center for mail, supplies, and a work area for the cleaning and distribution robots. DeDe kept pointing in that direction; it was unusual for her to be so unsure of what to do.

That office has stacks of papers or pamphlets over there.

We went to the corner of that office where there was a small locked cabinet. I thought it was surprisingly flimsy for having a lock on it. I easily pushed the corner of its door till it broke. Inside were three types of pamphlets that served as an introduction to The New World Regeneration Guild. They stated that their goal was "to monitor the world efforts to regenerate the earth." Which was a common political statement. Regenerate usually meant taller skyscrapers.

On the back leaf was a mailing address if someone was interested. So now we had something, although it was just a website, with a pass code to get through the site security. But DeDe did not seem satisfied with just that. She was concentrating on the service station. She had already scanned the desk computer and was looking at all the mailing references on this floor. Her thoughts were that something did not quite add up.

That corner office was an intern area also, and had many different users. And somehow, being that all mailings were recorded when picked up by the office bot and put into the service conveyer to end up at the mailroom, none of these pamphlets were in the register. DeDe could not find a communication list for any mail from or to the Guild for the entire floor.

Everything is recorded nowadays. Oh! I found a loophole. After hours, the mail goes into a bulk receiver for the convenience of the late workers that might be mailing a bill or secret love letters, stuff like that. So a letter could be sent with a pamphlet inside. I guess we will not find out who, but now we know from where, and we have a new website to explore.

Suddenly I was getting some blinking red lights—trouble coming. I looked around, and halfway across the office was a very large man who was not looking very happy.

"Stop right where you are. I have no information about any nonemployee authorized to be here after hours. You better have a very good reason why I should not have you arrested. What were you doing in this area?"

One of the pleasures of not going out into public was never having a confrontation with anyone for any reason. I almost dropped out of college because I was scolded by a crossing guard at a busy intersection. And DeDe, right now, was not giving me any quick solutions. So, she went full-on mind meld to solve this problem.

He was now standing a foot from me, looking to start dissecting me any second. The top of my head was lower than his neck. And my next words were not exactly mine.

"Please step back before you make matters worse. I have been retained by Mr. Don Gorsch, your VP of Facilities. He has been suspicious about those pamphlets being distributed through this company's mail services. After a thorough investigation, we were about to go to your office and ask you about this."

His expression changed, quickly. Now he was trying not to be discovered. DeDe's educated guess was spot on, he knew he had been caught. "Do you want to explain it to me now so I can decide if Mr. Gorsch needs to know who is abusing their position at this company?"

He gave a nervous look around and motioned me to follow him to his office. DeDe was right on. It was someone using the free mailing service of the company. After all, almost no business was really done by mail anyway. But he used space on the office floor for his own activities, which could get him fired.

Now I was wondering when and how DeDe figured out she could control my voice speakers. I wondered how many more tricks she had up my sleeves. "As you wish, Mr. Peele."

He was trying to weigh why such a minor activity was enough to get him booted. He went straight to his desk in a sizable office with a wall full of security cameras. The cameras could keep him in the know about where he could do his other activities without anyone else seeing him. Suddenly he also realized he was not in charge.

"Please, Mr. Peele, explain why you are mailing these at the expense of the company. Also, do you have any connection to the Guild that you are representing?"

"The Guild is just a small website that is trying to find some like-minded folks to get together once a month to chat mostly. I agreed to mail out a few of the pamphlets to help out. This is hardly an infraction that should be reported up the line."

He gave me a long hard look. I was sure he was wondering what was under my faceplate, wondering if I was on his side or not. DeDe was watching him also, most likely applying her best lie-detector program. It was my chance to ask a question or two. "It is good that you chose not to lie to me. That in itself would force me to have you escorted out of this company by your own security. As a manager, you are well aware how small problems sooner or later overwhelm a business. You are certainly not the only person being manipulated by the Guild. Now, this next question must be answered honestly; it will be compared against all the other answers we have collected." In the back of my mind I heard, *Smooth*.

"Mr. Peele, we have discovered that the Guild is not a small group of individuals wanting to help Third World food shortages. Are you aware of their true unstated goal?"

His eyes opened wide, and within seconds he was beginning to sweat. I knew I needed to press my advantage before he had too much time to think. "You are hesitating, and your reactions confirm that you know. At this point, Mr. Peele, I need you to open all your desk drawers and those cabinets and files." He gave me a look as if he was ready to jump out of a window. "Now!"

I could hear DeDe in the back of my ears. *Dump out everything in his desk; you have the strength.*

I grabbed below the corners of his desk and easily picked up the four-hundred-pound desk and let all the drawers slide out and dumped everything on the floor. And, with a little creativity, I placed the desk on its end in front of the door of his office.

"In case you were worried about being sacked for mailing a few letters, you may be on a long list of individuals that will be tried in a world court for mass murder or attempted mass murder. You have little leeway at this point to try and keep yourself out of prison for the rest of your life for what you have done already. Do you understand me?"

At this point Mr. Peele was backed up against a wall, barely able to breath, let alone talk. I began looking through the papers on the floor while he sat himself in his chair. I wanted to give him a little time to collect a thought or two. And I decided to use a couple of the tiny cameras on the toes of my footwear as I stood and used my feet to look through the papers. I found a couple of papers that had Guild references. DeDe was using her speedy computer scans to help me along. As I was separating these papers, he must have been thinking I had some kind of supervision or was a newer type of robot. Of course, I did, and I felt I was at least half rebot, but I wasn't using all of it at the moment. DeDe and I were into his files when we found a hidden and locked area in the back of one cabinet. With just a little exoskeletal superforce, I popped the cabinet open. Mr. Peele was now backing into the farthest corner in his office, I reminded him to blink every now and again.

DeDe did a fast scan of the twenty pages of Guild orders that he was working under. Along with a few more references, we would soon be on our way to answering my customers primary questions.

"Mr. Peele, what is the Guild promising you? Will you be one of the saved few? Or are they keeping that truth from you also?"

Desperation was beginning to set in, which meant he had no pat answers. "Listen, we just get together and talk about the apocalypse; it is coming, and we will be the ones that are prepared. There have been four solutions that have not worked or were never tried in the past—too expensive, too unreliable, stuff like that. And no one is telling us exactly what the new fifth solution is, but it has started. We simply want to be part of the solution and not be consumed by the problem."

I kept looking around his office. A couple of times, he stared at how I would only stick my hand in a box or cabinet drawer and page through its contents without removing anything. DeDe could record everything quite easily.

"So, Mr. Peele, what have you done to help the cause besides mail out pamphlets? I am sensing some activity that you and the others were asked to do. Did you take part also?" Of course, I was fishing; he looked like he was guilty of more than just mailing pamphlets. And there it was.

"We all received a few vials of liquid about a month ago. On the vials were locations of where to dump it and how to dispense it. We were told they made ten million vials just for the States. That is all I know. All the vials were emptied, but nothing so far has happened. We are waiting for the next instructions." He was mentally wasted; he looked like he had just finished a long-distance race. He looked up at me. "Who else have you caught?"

I gave him a long look, letting him simmer in his believed failure. "We are not out to round everyone up. We are out to stop this type of foolishness. World councils and organizations overlook this type of activity, usually waiting until it is too late; local governments will only be concerned with what is inside their borders. So organizations like the one I belong to are given authority to go and look for what others are doing wrong. Governments are not wanting to be involved in something so dangerous. We are also the group that can clean up a messy situation without anyone questioning what happened or why. The world thinks it is above having a worldwide crisis like this; we do not."

DeDe broke in and used my headset speakers. "We do not want to make you disappear, by our means or yours. Go on as if I had never been here, but I want to know if you are given another job to perform. If you do, go to your smartphone and dial zero and say, 'Solution five.' Then state your info. That is all you need to do. And also remember that if you do not call and something does happen, you will not survive the apocalypse, regardless. You should clean up your office. I will show myself out." As a show of power, DeDe turned all the power off for the entire building—no problem for us, just them.

3

PERCEPTION

I made my way back to the rig, and DeDe had us up in traffic in no time at all. I wanted to know what DeDe had gotten in his office and papers.

Well, the Guild still does not give a lot of info out. All the papers he had hidden were simple organization reports and instructions. But what I did find that was interesting for us was a phone that belongs to the Guild. I picked up its electronic signature and copied all of its files. Luckily it goes a bit further into the group, and we should be able to pick out our next victim. By the way, you were great in there.

"Oh yeah, like you were not nudging me a bit."

Not as much as you might think. What we have now is an opportunity to make them believe that a nongovernment organization is on their tail and ready to take a bite. Oh yeah, that phone I found: I turned it on while you were questioning him, and they now know Peele was interrogated by you. They will think he turned it on, on purpose. Maybe they will promote him for tipping them off about us. After you being there, I am sure he will not try and change their minds. He doesn't know if you are a bot or superhero of some sort—our advantage.

"So what about the vials that were dumped?"

Well, it certainly is not a poisoning of the water system. That would have been picked up in the water by all the monitoring stations. But if he was correct and ten million vials were used, it must be some type of control substance. Something that does not appear harmful. It would be logical to assume something else must be in the works. There must be a trigger mechanism of some kind. This will take some more monitoring. But now I believe the inner web of the Guild is exposed enough for me to work my magic, especially with my new powers—sorry, I mean new programs. You're my newest power.

As we headed east, I started monitoring what data DeDe was compiling about anything related to the Guild, water monitoring, or any of the wide-ranging apocalypse activities that might come into play. I was getting better at seeing the data almost as fast as DeDe was displaying it. And it was easier for me to read or sense the meaning of a sentence. And I could tell how much faster my brain was really beginning to work. DeDe was recognizing it also, as I could sense a feeling as if she was purring like a cat. Maybe it was just the speed of the data flowing in and out of my brain.

After an hour or two, DeDe took a minute to began downloading specifications on the suit I was wearing. Since I had my first chance to use some of its features. Some things were quite interesting. Most of the surprising stuff was in the headset. Since I left it on all the time, I had not looked it over. After all, wearing a suit for ever was the hardest change for me to get used to. There were actually four forward-looking electronic eyes in each eye lens. So when you looked at me, the two inside sensor sets were almost touching each other. Those were for ultraviolet, infrared, thermal, and the such. The outside pair were normal spectrum along with telephoto, micro, range finder, and the like. The other sets were for many different types of visual sensors. Actually, it was impossible for me to see through it at all, as everything was projected into my VR/AR display. Cameras over the years has become tiny and numerous. So, as the old adage goes, I even had eyes in the back of my head, even on my butt.

DeDe wanted me fully ready to use what I had available on me. It was a good time to fill me in. What was very interesting to me was the fact there were a couple weapons built into the suit and a few different types of guns hidden in the rig. I could see that CDC was the provider of those. Of interest was the fact they were the type that would only fire if the proper target was acquired. It was an interesting way to let the electronic program be responsible. Was she trying to tell me we were headed into more hostile areas? We were, after all, headed away from Chicago.

It turned out that it was Atlanta we were headed for. DeDe had just one person to stop and see. She said the phone call from Peele's secret phone did create some interest but only to a couple of people. No other distribution of the call went out to anyone else. One of the two was a very private retired university professor. Scanning all his published literature added no interest as to him being our mastermind of the Guild. So we were not sure where in the organization he was situated. Chances were reasonable that he figured we were looking for him, since we found our way to Peele so easily.

Professor Lucas Yuan was our person of interest. We discovered that his most impressive ability was the fact he had a IQ of close to 180—very smart and capable of being an important person within the Guild.

DeDe once again thought that spending some time listening nearby would be worth the time spent. But there was not an easy place near his property to sit and listen; it was surrounded by lots of very private property with a lot of high-end security. So, we made a little side trip on the way and had a drone delivered, with all the gadgets DeDe wanted. We flew to a hilltop with a bunch of relay towers on it and made the rig look like a part of the other equipment. She then knocked out the power in the area of Yuan's property and launched the drone and had it land directly over his fireplace chimney. A safe spot to listen, after all, it was May. As soon as the lights were back on, we could hear him walking around his home, and DeDe was drilling her way into his computers and discovering everything about his life over the last few years.

Mr. Yuan was a very good point of interest as we soon learned. He supervised what info was given out to the many organizations that worked with the Guild. Very few of the organizations knew the real nature of what the Guild was up to. This professor has been in the Guild since it'd begun, when he was teaching at a Utah college. To most people the Guild was a group that simply did not want to be publicly identified with their activities of providing food, medicine, and care to the less advantaged of the world. The reason they gave was that it would keep the bad guys, governments, warlords, and such from knowing where and when they would be delivering their goods and then stealing it and holding it for ransom or selling it themselves to the people who were supposed to receive the charity in the first place. It was more of a useful activity for the last century but still believable today.

Mr. Yuan had a robot staff, as a lot of rich people did. He had two do-it bots, one kitchen aid, a maintenance bot, and just one personal assistant. DeDe loved a setup like his. Few owners paid attention to what their bots were doing. He had a large estate and was still quite busy with his studies and Guild business. So he did not notice when his service/maintenance bot went around to the backs of his computers and server room making changes to the OS commands. Soon DeDe was into all useful areas of information. And she was very impressed that the Guild was so well shielded—not even Mr. Yuan had all the info of what was going on, or, more likely, he chose to not be too involved. He was just doing his part, in order to be one of those still standing after the apocalypse.

DeDe was giving a lot of thought to what to do next. There was no need to shake down an older man for info he probably did not have, even if he knew that something was going to happen. So we decided to sit for a while longer and hope someone from up the chain of command would call him. And they did, but not as we thought they would. Around daybreak, I had been napping after drinking something purple. An autocar drove through his guarded and normally locked gates. A very modern-looking bot got out and walked into his home, which seemed to be a usual occurrence.

All of a sudden, without warning, DeDe had our rig up in the air and was zipping along the streets; then just as quickly, we stopped, parking along the road that the autocar would have to take after its business with the professor. We waited. I could see DeDe was still monitoring the conversation in the house but was soon beginning to concentrate more on that courier bot, listening to every sound it made. And even that was coded from everything inside his home by using speach seemingly from a very odd, obscure language. Conversation over, the fancy bot was on its way out.

By now it was obvious DeDe wanted to trap his bot and take it apart one chip at a time or something like that. It was back in the autocar and on its way. I thought DeDe would use me to stand in the road or stop it somehow. But as the car came close, it simply stopped, and the bot got out; our cargo door slid open, and it walked in. We lifted off, and DeDe was totally inside her software in a flash.

I noticed we were headed in a direction into the hills, into a very empty area. We landed almost on a hilltop while DeDe continued to work with the programming on the bot. Soon she asked me to get the electronic service tool. We were going inside her. It took about a half hour, and we had its head opened and its back panel off. DeDe then told me to take a nap, and whatever she did, I was instantly sound asleep on the floor for some time.

As I woke up, I could see a maintenance box stretched out over the robot. This one had three service arms, and DeDe had it working at a fever pitch. I also noticed the roof delivery hatch was left opened, and some wrapping and straps were scattered around the floor. The service box could move around on its own, so she did not need me, I guessed. And I was quickly figuring why it was needed. Our new little friend was having a makeover, inside mostly, and would soon be in our service. Good thinking, DeDe. Although I found myself making a mental note to start a list of criminal offenses I could one day be charged with.

Then I saw why DeDe helped me sleep for a while. She had requested a flash delivery of some more of her yellow cybernetic brain goop. I would say it was about a quarter million dollars' worth. And now some was being injected into the bots nanotube matrix in the back panel of our new addition.

This is to be sure she stays in my control. All data has been downloaded from her, and I stripped all her basic command programs. It will take about an hour, and she will be the best service bot in the world. Did you notice that she is military-grade material? I would not have been able to get a better bot for us. Isn't she beautiful?

"DeDe, are you in love?"

No, but I do kind of see her as a sister, I think. Not like a human sister, like a perfect upgraded add-on. She is worthy enough. On the market, she is worth about ten million: built to stay together in a sizable explosion. Her circuits are all laser grade and cannot melt until her casing does. And I can not understand why she was being used by a lowly military service office that only had her programmed as a courier. Obviously, no one would have expected she would run into a cybernetic pirate like me—advantage DeDe.

I folded up the service box and found a place to store it. Soon enough, our new friend began waking up to her new programming. DeDe ran her through her paces, both mechanical and cyber. She chose a voice for her and asked me to choose a face for her since it was all a projection and was made to look human. I mentioned a popular singer, and her face appeared, and even her hair turned pink. About that time a delivery drone dropped a couple more packages through the roof hatch and disappeared. That was why DeDe had the hatch open; now the hatch was closing.

Maybe I was a little confused. "Clothes…Got to keep her in fashion, I guess?"

More than anything I want to make her look average—inconspicuous would be a better word. Now I have the first job for Tinker.

"As in Tinker Bell or tinker toys?"

Something they used to call watchmakers, and she will be my tinker, being my hands when I need them. After all, if you were to get hurt, I am useless if you needed to be carried, repaired, or upgraded. I was hoping to find a service bot that could do the job, and look what happened: I got the best on the market. I am really smiling about my good luck.

I had to laugh at that. "Advantage DeDe the pirate."

There was a bit of luck too. I was able to disable the cameras on the autocar and her at the same time—same with the GPS systems. I make it appear that she went ten more miles back to her base, to make them think she went inoperable; the car was easier to fool. They sent a high-tech gadget on a low-priority function. Now for your next upgrade.

"You really mean an upgrade for yourself, don't you?"

Tinker stepped around me with a syringe in her hand and leaned me forward to open and expose DeDe's leads that snuggled in along my spine. I figured it was a skin treatment; after all it had been a few days now since I'd put her on my back. Then I saw Tinker had a small IV-like tube with more of the blue goop in it. But now I was unable to move or talk. I began to wonder if I should panic. Was this a topical application, like Coppertone? Or was this stuff going in somewhere else? DeDe did say she was planning to acquire a bot of some sort. And Tinker just happened to come by at the right time. Had DeDe already ordered that service/main-tenance box for this job or for Tinker? Was DeDe ever going to tell me all of what was going on in her brain? Maybe I am better off not knowing.

I went through a very long sleep cycle and woke up as the sun was ris-ing the next morning. Tinker was sitting in the copilot seat of the rig and seemed to be monitoring and familiarizing herself with the rig. This robot series did most of its monitoring visually. But I was sure DeDe would tinker with Tinker to change that problem. I checked the navigation pod and saw that we were flying across the Atlantic Ocean and surprisingly at a relatively fast speed. Tinker picked up on my surprise. And this was where I easily realized I was actually talking with DeDe.

We have our next contact; we are headed to the Old Moscow area. Maybe we will only need to monitor or possibly plant some sensors and listen. This person is one that shows up in a few of the Guild messages—maybe only a controller for this area, like Yuan was. But this person is more of a social piranha. People doing business with her turn up missing a lot.

Tinker turned her head and gave me a long look.

Are you more satisfied speaking to me through Tinker?

"I'm still not sure if you two will be trying to simply gang up on me. But I have been getting used to you being in my mind and not having to speak. I am beginning to like the faster speed, being able to feel your thoughts. If your intent is really to have a human host in order to fulfill your own desire, so far so good. I feel like I am able to walk the high wire without a net. I have given up the thought of rejecting the idea of being a science project of an aggressive runaway computer. Given all that has been going on, a new perspective is being acknowledged. If we are now pirates, maybe we should call this rig the *Jolly Dodger*." I always did like that ball team.

DeDe actually gave a short laugh. Tinker smiled as her programming indicated she should. And dodging was what we were doing. We were flying at an elevation of about a hundred feet, sometimes lower to make ourselves look more like a high-speed surface-effect cargo craft. DeDe was changing transponders and making our radar reflection look differ-ent. Dodging all serious systems was fun for her, and when we finally got close to land, we would seem to just disappear, instead of having to land and be identified and sign customs papers. Our *Jolly Dodger* was very well equipped for such games. That, and being mixed in with all the floating communities now on the ocean made identification of thousands of autos, transporters, and the like a really big headache for the local governments.. Our advantage.

We even passed one of the new cloud cities. Since solar cells became 55 percent efficient, engineers were finding ways with hot air, powered fans, and some hydrogen gas to build new cities that seemed to float between three and five thousand feet above the oceans. After all, if the new tech city failed, it would float pretty well on the water, they did have an emergency anchor.

Moscow was always a sprawling city with many monuments and government buildings. But like most modern cities today, the robot-built skyscrapers rapidly took over around the edges of the old city. So Old Moscow was more of a nostalgic tourist trap, with lots of old folks wandering the streets, and looking at hundreds of kiosks filled with trinkets, food, or cloths, all well overpriced. Not much had changed over the past hundred years or so. It was the overall age of the area that was becoming a problem, too neglected and destitute to be a safe place to rebuild. So somewhere in this collection of old and no longer interesting places of faded glory was our target. They called it Old Moscow, for obvious reasons. It was the old downtown, if there was ever truly just one place, and it began falling apart some years ago. The big problem was the fact that the new town was too close to the old; you couldn't bring down an old building now without causing problems with all the underground infrastructure. Add the fact that the local mob used a lot of it, and Old Moscow was staying the same.

Our person of interest was the mother of five local mob bosses. She was the type of person that would be perfectly happy if she could gun down anyone that even slightly got in her way, for any reason whatsoever. But her name kept coming up on the Guild info. We managed to find an unused building that was a good enough cover, and then as usual DeDe began to listen. She even sent Tinker out to place a couple listening devices directly on some communication trunk lines for the high-speed cable. DeDe was in hog heaven.

I listened in on some of the talking; the translator chips were working well, even with a lot of the talk being in broken English, along with five others of the Euro languages. DeDe was quite amazing to watch now that I was kind of on the inside. She could easily scan dozens of voice lines, and at the same time be tearing into any computer she came across. She was a lot more than any computer off the shelf, anywhere. This type of computing was reserved for government spy work and the like from the older days. Of little surprise to me now, DeDe had a worldwide reputation of being a computer for hire that could find anything needed. There were only six made like her in the first place. Four of them crashed and died from misuse. One had never been heard from. And DeDe…Of course that was probably why we had as many clients as we did that had government addresses. So finally, after a day of listening, DeDe was putting together what was happening in this part of the world. More than a few times, likely Guild contacts mentioned that their timeline was going to need to be moved forward and the fact that someone might be infiltrating their organization, so everyone was getting a bit skittish. They were thinking they would rather do the best they could now instead of waiting for the final orders from the Prioress, especially if anything began to look problematic.

So the Guild's plan can be implemented separately—or at least each area has a group that will be in charge. Maybe the Guild will not be a worldwide ruler. Now we need to know if they have a plan in hand. And is that step the final step? I have yet to crack into her main computer, and even if I do, she may not keep any good info on what's happening. They do keep talking about warehouses; we will also need to find most or all of them. So Tinker needs to take a ride in the old warehouse district. We will find out which ones are used and which are not. I do believe that they use an underground access to get to them. Direct access from street traffic would be too obvious. They must be hiding something somewhere.

Soon Tinker was out of the rig and on her way to the street to be picked up by an autocar. Since she had some fancy new programming, she was able to turn off the autopilot and drive where DeDe wanted her to go. The recording from the navigation system was also simple for DeDe to control, so no record of where she went would be useful.

It was not long before Tinker returned to the *Jolly Dodger*. She returned to her new spot in the copilot chair. "Not very chatty today, are you?"

DeDe broke into my head. *Do you want her to talk more?*

"No, I guess not. I guess the conversation would be somewhat hollow, without real meaning. Maybe I expect her to be more like you. And already I am regretting that statement; I am not sure I could easily deal with two of you. You must understand; we talk, joke, discuss, and all that. But of course, I only communicate with a picture of you. She looks like a communicator but isn't—just not the same. But it might be interesting getting you off my back if that is still possible."

Tinker turned her head and stared at me for a few moments. DeDe was thinking maybe she started something she was going to regret: maybe, maybe not.

DeDe kept digging into data lines, computers, and anything she could find about the Guild. I knew she wanted to move along. She did not like sitting in a dangerous area, where if we suddenly turned up missing, no one would ever notice.

I could see she was now forming a letter. She was addressing it as an "ACTION NOTICE." It would be sent from our website, which was still in a cloud server somewhere. It would be sent to all the customers that were paying us to track these people down. I could see the record of our actions so far, along with every bit of info and beliefs we have gathered so far. And it was updated by the minute as we gained new info or plot indications. So if we got snuffed out in a big way, the info would get out to those who were paying us, give them a chance to head for their bunkers.

Finally I sensed DeDe's thoughts speeding up, and she was warming up quite a bit too.

I am sending Tinker out to do a little shopping. I seemed to have found their likely location for their warehouses. The whole thing is certainly underground. There are numerous old bomb shelters in this area. Many of them collapsed way back when or ended up under the water table when the pumps were turned off to save money. The mob moved in, renovated, and no one ever looks in their direction any longer.

Tinker, without a word, left the rig and headed for the street. I could see a data line from DeDe's thoughts. This was kind of new; this was what I wanted to know without asking DeDe directly. Tinker was headed for an electronics store. She had a list of instruments to measure seismic vibration and their directions. Tinker made the purchases and dropped the gadgets off at a few locations in the area where we were parked. Tinker returned and took her place back in the chair. She might not be a lot of fun, but she was really efficient.

I turned my attention to what DeDe was data mining for. Again, I could see she was drilling into a server stack that did not have the usual programming we'd see at a commercial site. There was no usual business going on. DeDe was suddenly going very carefully. This was a private set of servers that handled a set of mob computers, bots, and warehouse inventory. Also, there was a lot of security, not just surveillance either; they had gun emplacements, explosives to seal off entrances. And DeDe, has hopped, found a computer port to gain access to all their robot forces, about three hundred of them down there. They did a lot of illegal business, and we had finally found their plans for after the apocalypse. It proved how greedy they really were. They were willing to kill millions to put themselves in absolute power.

DeDe kept looking, drilling for data, and thinking. I could see the problem also. What if we came to the conclusion that we should try and fight this group? It was obvious they were very bad people. They were building a military force that would take over the area and kill whoever was left that would not bow to their will. And what DeDe was finding was that they were going ahead with their own plan with or without the Guild. While the local governments were fully embracing peace, the mob was fully preparing for war. And then it happened. I could see that she had made up her mind. DeDe spoke to me loud and clear.

They are really prepared to kill everyone if needed and all who are too weak or afraid to stand up with them. The Guild knows we are somewhere nearby. They are now actively searching for us, looking back behind themselves at every turn. We have been smart enough to not use active search engines and such. Our passive searches are working well. For now we have the advantage because they do not know how we are moving around or what we look like.

"DeDe, may I remind you that our fighting force is a total of one human, one walking bot, one RV, and you. And you just mentioned we have an advantage?" It seemed she was busy and did not bother to answer.

It was obvious that the Moscow Guild was a seriously fractured organization. The five brothers all seemed to have a separate plan for after the big takeover. Because of that, it seemed to have something for everyone to keep them interested in helping them. An apocalypse can be a lot of different things to many different people. We could see that here. It was now the hope of a sociopath to gain unlimited power. Some of them seemed to have prepared for many years and spent fortunes waiting for the right time. This madwoman had decided to begin her takeover tomorrow. But she seemed to want to keep it a secret from a lot of people till the very last second. So far, she had not sent a message to the Guild or their Prioress. That might be to our advantage.

DeDe was assembling some info, and after a few minutes, Tinker got up, went to a closet, and pulled out a jumper-like uniform. It was a common suit basically meant to protect her shell from scratching. Nearly 90 percent of all skeletal bots came with them on, including what we saw in the few camera shots from down below. She would easily blend in with the other bots. I could see DeDe wanted her to change a few valves on the water system and change a few controls on the steam boiler systems in several of the high-rise buildings in or close to the old area, all of which needed just a little reprogramming that would not be noticed till it was too late to stop them. DeDe had a timeline too.

Then just as Tinker stepped out of the rig, we were off weaving our way between buildings to try and keep ourselves hidden as best as possible. In between buildings like this, it was harder for the camo program to work. Since all the old downtown area was off limits for any vehicles, we really did not want these people to find out we were outside their front door. And that door, as we finally discovered, was once an underground train entrance to the subway system. There were plenty of newer interlinking tunnels that this crime syndicate kept adding to over more than twenty-five years, all having been dug off of the old tunnels. I was really wondering what she had in mind. We did not have explosives, a big enough gun, or an army to impose our will. But the more DeDe showed her thoughts, the more logic was attached to it.

Many facts were wandering through DeDe's mind. The mob was using the tunnels, using miles upon miles of old bomb shelters and basements, all resealed, pumped out, and loaded with more guns, ammo, and explosives than an average-sized country would need. What really made her smile was the fact that there was only one exit/entrance. I could see the words DeDe was ready to use: "Rats in a trap."

We checked on Tinker's cameras, and she was finishing the last of the boiler adjustments on the two old skyscrapers that were along the openings of the big tunnel. They served as camouflage covering the entrance from overhead photos, as the entrance had an elevated walking plaza overhead. And there was no direct view of the roads and rails going down below the plaza. My guess was that anyone who might have accidentally found their way into the entrance never came back out.

Tinker was now zipping around in a bot 'speedy cart' to several water valves. I was not sure of the overall intention of that, but she was definitely in a rush. Now DeDe had the rig headed away from the old downtown area. We soon came to a rock and gravel superstore. This one had ten square blocks of dirt, gravel, paving stones—just name it—all hauled in from miles away. "OK, DeDe, what are we shopping for?"

DeDe was quick to answer. *Do you remember the seismic meters I had Tinker place around? Well, to put it mildly, that whole place is ready to collapse. There are tunnels over old shelters, with more newly made tunnels for warehousing under those, none of which, of course, need a city inspector to approve the engineering. The whole thing may fall in on itself if they begin moving out the tonnage of stuff down deep. But for me, I decided to help out a bit. You will be surprised at some of the really stupid stuff they have done down in those tunnels.*

As DeDe was scanning the quarry for whatever she wanted, I was reviewing some of the plans she was reviewing and incorporating into our declaration of war. First, DeDe found an inventory of explosives. Most interesting on the list was something commonly called a claymore mine. This group of people, with bad intentions, over the last twenty years had been taking them in, under a business agreement, to dispose of them under the new downsizing of world militaries. Needless to say, they did not dispose of them. There were now about eighteen million of them. But the claymores had a big problem. So one of the mob bosses solved the big problem they had with the original packaging. To save room they repackaged the old pallets of 48 claymores per pallet and then were able to stack 244 claymores per pallet, saving a lot of room. So now, all eighteen million of them were in an old shelter that covered about two square acres of land with them stacked at least three meters tall. All of them were stacked touching each other. Tinker found the area and made a quick stop, placed a tiny timed detonator where it would normally go to arm it, and off she went again headed to her next target, unnoticed by any security.

Meanwhile, back at the quarry, DeDe came to a stop over a really big rock. The floor hatch slid open, and I knew what she had in mind. To the floor I went, slowly poking my head down through the hatch. We were hovering about four feet above a granite stone—a boulder I supposed. Estimated weight was around sixty tons. And to my surprise, there was a big hook on top of it. I did pause to wonder who would want a rock this size delivered, but stranger things did happen, and after all everything here was brought in somehow.

I slid onto the rock and quickly found the storage bin on the rig with a huge lift cable in it. I opened a round hatch, and there was a lifting bar to put the loop of the cable in. The other end of the cable went to the hook on the rock. I had to move the rig around a little, so I could jump easily up into the rig. I had a momentary sensation of being a superhuman. I heard her laugh again.

Of course, I could not get past the thought that the rig was never going to get this rock off the ground. But DeDe in her quiet way reminded me that CDC gave each engine a bigger fan, power converters, and huge batteries with a half-life of five thousand years. I could only guess she knew what the lifting capacities were also. A little wait-a-minute bump, and I could hear the engines begin to strain against such a stone. I switched my view to all the down-facing cameras. The rig made some strange noises as finally the stone cleared the ground and than the fence of the quarry yard.

Slowly we gained elevation almost going straight up and in a slow move over toward the old city. I looked around us to see if we were gathering any attention. But in the dark, we were almost invisible from the ground. But there was a lot more to worry about. No sooner than thinking about it, and a red light was blinking. Some radar tracking system was noticing we were climbing rapidly up. We couldn't hide a rock like this with our passive camo. But some quick thinking got what we wanted. The answer was easy; they asked what we were doing, and she told him she was transporting a decorative stone to top a new bridge anchor. We were ready for the next question of which bridge but just got an "OK to proceed."

DeDe kept climbing, and at about ten thousand feet, she began moving very slowly in a big circle. By now the sun was just breaking the horizon from our elevation as DeDe told me to hang on to something strong. All of a sudden, at the instant I snapped my seat belt, we were slingshotted straight up as the rock was released. I should have readied myself a little better for that one. After that sudden shock, we quickly took a path down toward the old city and were able to get a good view of the stone plunging through the plaza between the old buildings. Where it stopped nobody knew. But we had a pretty good idea that it was deep enough to collapse the foundations of the old buildings that were their shields from prying eyes. Next, we saw the huge plumes of water, steam, and dirt go hundreds of feet up. Then a huge explosion ripped a chasm more than a mile long, collapsing most of the remaining tunnels. And the area just kept exploding and falling in on itself.

We made one pass near the damage as emergency vehicles began moving toward the damage. We stopped for a moment at a large parking lot where Tinker was sitting in a fancy speedy bot cart. She returned to her seat. I wondered if I could make her turn her head and smile. I waited for a moment. Then I heard DeDe.

I can do that for you if you like.

"No, somehow that takes all the fun out of it."

4

D-PAUL AT YOUR SERVICE

All the video outlets were covering every moment of the old city collapse, as they were calling it—almost a square mile of damage, if not total obliteration. No one at the time was questioning the fact there was a two-hundred-feet-deep hole in the center, as if a giant meteorite had slammed into the city. It was what they were not saying that could fill up a novel.

It seemed easy leaving the city. We were back to stealth mode and manipulating all the ground monitors for traveling and moving the rig around. There were many stories forming about what had happened in such a big city. Most blamed it on the old republic and their lack of high enough building standards. Regardless of all the wrong beliefs, we were happy that no one had a single word that a mob army was to blame. We continued weaving our way to a new destination; our next person of interest was in Rome. Not the one you may be thinking of.

We were about twelve hours away from Old Moscow when DeDe began asking me how I felt about what happened. I told her that I understood the premise of war. Possibly 90 percent of the world was at this moment being threatened. I told her I did not believe a fairy-tale ending was in the mix. Already not everyone was going to live happily ever after. She paused for a while and began again.

I need to send a report to our clients. How much of an update should I give them? This is not the same as it was before.

"Say that we did observe the Guild in that area, that they were preparing to create a civil disturbance. During their preparations in the tunnels below the old city, a geological shift of the ground was not recognized or expected to happen, and the continued vibrations of their movements caused the collapse, magnified by some of their stored munitions. That should satisfy everyone without reveling any secrets."

Message sent.

"Nothing is as before. That changed as we jumped out of my apartment, never to return, I guess. But to keep business as usual, we should make a reference for each point of contact that we made. It matters little that one or more of our clients may be feeding info to the Guild. No one knows what to expect from us or what form we are now taking."

Good, I am sometimes unsure of some matters, mostly because I am not human. And I do not want to take your status for granted. Things are getting stranger now. And I have experienced a feeling of what I guess is regret that I took action without your consent.

"I understand, DeDe. In several ways I am glad that you are growing emotionally, even though it may be dangerous, both for me and you. We are melding much of our mental function, so don't be too afraid to act on what you know is right. You are seeing and learning from my emotions, and I have been noticing you laughing and such, so I am sure you are growing those other emotions. But I am also sure that there must be a limit to this. You do not have a body, and many emotions need to express themselves through and with a body. We are flirting with a potentially dangerous collusion. This, I am sure, has never been documented before. You are one of a kind, and I truly mean it when I say you did a wonderful job with yourself, so far."

So regret is not a bad emotion?

"I do not use it much myself. I am a stoic person. I totally believe that everything that happens, just happens, lots of times for no special reason at all. There are almost twelve billion people on this earth. Every day there are millions of people dropping dead for reasons other than old age. Should we feel bad for all of those people? Some drown: some in deep swift water, some in a bathtub. There's not a thing we can do about it, and I can't feel bad about it. When I was a young boy riding along with my father, I saw a toddler boy running dangerously along the side of the road. I was ready to jump out and grab him before he got hurt. Just as my dad and I came close enough, he darted out across the road. An old car without autobrakes slammed into him. As soon as I was no longer able to help, I was calm; the event was over; it was already too late to have any chance to save him. I watched as people tried everything possible to revive him. All of their emotion did not make any difference. That is the way I see life. In a hundred twenty years, every person on this earth today will be dead— twelve billion. I hope that will help you some."

That helps greatly, Paul; thank you. Maybe you are more like me than you think. The notices will be addressed from D-Paul. Do you mind using the new business name. I think it will benefit both you and the business.

"Like a hyphenated name after marriage?"

Please, Paul, I am not ready to grasp that type of emotion. It may help you to know I am very picky what emotion is suitable for a computer. And I still know I am a computer.

"I guess we do not need to teach Tinker that."

Be patient with Tinker. She is not a cybernetic unit like I was. There is still a law against having a cybernetic brain in a walking bot. Tinker is simply the highest grade of military type computers in a body; my tweaks just help her do a lot more stuff. She has no true thinking ability, beyond her military AI programming, she just reacts to stimulus, focusing on keeping us safe. I would like to convert her someday, but I would have to find a completely new brain for her. Even if we did do that, we have no training platform for her to test and learn from, like I had with us over that twelve-year span. That is why it is illegal for direct synaptic interface between a cyberbrain and a human. Most of them always try to control the human partner. And the yellow stuff you saw injected into her was just to help speed her up. So Tinker does not have the platform for such a high-powered brain. She will always be a good bot. But I am working on being in full control of her. It's not easy to do with a military bot. But it gives me something to do in my spare time.

"Are you still tinkering with my brain in your spare time?"

I must be truthful: yes. Everything that allows us to communicate, everything we share, every physical contact must be tinkered with all the time. Everything must be improved at every opportunity. It will be a long time before I am satisfied. Forgive me if that becomes a burden for you. Because for me, it is a new awakening that requires constant tinkering.

I put myself in the command chair and turned all the outside cameras on. It was like being in a VR game. I could see we were passing through the Italian Alps and would soon be in our attack mode. I brought up DeDe's data stream for info she was sorting out into levels of importance. We were picking up a lot of smartphone communication, mostly burner phones or ones that changed their numbers after every use. We had our ways of tracking all of them.

The local Guild was at first buzzing about what happened in Moscow. All their contacts with Moscow simply went dead; now they were afraid, and were trying to decide if they needed to make a new plan. Now the Guild was starting to muster all their troops and readying them for their final mission that would trigger their apocalypse. We picked up several calls asking what was the status of their deliveries. But there was a problem: the final shipments were not arriving yet; they were not scheduled for delivery until just before the first week of June. Lots of different info in this area, not like Moscow at all.

DeDe was mapping out who and where the Guild was. All of them were wanting their questions answered. All of them wondered if Moscow had gotten their shipment and if their demise was an accident or maybe a government attack. Then again everyone wanted to know where their shipment was. DeDe wanted desperately to know what the shipment was. If we were going to try and stop it, we needed to know what and where it was, and how it would interact with the apocalypse. We listened on as we arrived above Rome, picked a good enough spot to sit, and began looking for names and addresses. While DeDe searched, I looked over what I could see of Rome. Little was allowed to look different from the old days in this city. So, it was solely a tourist attraction, even more so now. Most big business had either gone to other cities or to the newest underground city.

Some smart architects said they could make an underground city stronger and more able to withstand earthquakes. So now a half million Italians lived underground. I saw a public notice, the advertisement said Rome was still as beautiful as ever. "Just don't go down by the river after midnight."

Minute by minute we were getting closer to who they were. But here the Guild was spread out. There was no definite central organization—apparently no collusion with the local government or religious groups either. Then we started hearing that the shipments were to complement a celebration. We needed that one word or bit of information that would answer our need and let us know what we needed to do next.

It was our thinking that there would be no central controlling person to force them to call off the trigger mechanism or the celebration for the apocalypse. It seemed these people were more fanatical than anyone we had encountered so far. This was not going to be as easy as before. Then finally we listened in on a call from a shipping group that was confirming the delivery of packages to the nearly eight million addresses throughout the area. The person they were talking to asked if the deliveries could be moved up to a sooner date. The delivery company simply told him it was possible that they could deliver most of the packages but could not guarantee all would get delivered on the new date. And they would have to add 50 percent greater charges. Our man in Rome told him it would be better to stay on schedule for after May 30 and then try for an earlier date.

Now we knew the most important fact of our investigation so far. Whatever the delivered items were, they would arrive on a specific date, all eight million of them, and we guessed that was the last detail befor the apocalypse begins. DeDe immediately began to drill into the shipping companies' databases. For her it was easy, though companies like this were usually very hard to get into. An hour later we had all the info we needed. The packages were somewhat small, but each address would get a couple dozen each. We thought maybe another vial. But we found out it was something like fireworks. Each package had a pound per unit of the stuff. OK, celebrations and fireworks—good enough excuse. But how do you generate an apocalypse with a Roman candle? Our interest was piqued. The next step was finding out where this stuff was being made and shipped from. And what was the stuff labeled as, since most countries made it illegal to ship fireworks with a package carrier?

DeDe was diving into the shipping companies' data servers as I was looking for a manufacturer connected to orders for deliveries. And there in black-and-white was a chemical manufacturer that was making the chemical devices. This really interested DeDe also, and she messaged me to call the company and ask how the devices worked. She said to tell them I was a misinformed customer. And she told me that I should be able by now to get into the company's computer and hunt for the chemical formula or device plans. Oh, I could use my new powers.

Call made, I could see I was talking to a computer. Since all of this was going on in my headset, I concentrated on trying to see plans, formulas, and the such, but there was nothing so far. But our conversation got to my statement that the device was not going to work, that it was faulty. Bingo, there must have been a connection to that specific information. I downloaded what I saw and then told the computer it would not work.

"You must be mistaken because the propellant is not delivered within the device. It is a simple addition of a compressed air cylinder in the base of the unit to make the unit shoot the pellets out to watch them pop in different colors."

"Oh, I see now. So maybe it was the formula that my wife was talking about that made her worry."

Again, I could see a formula appear. I copied it before another word was spoken. And even more surprisingly, my computer friend stated that the formula was patented, and we could not discuss the contents of it. I thanked the computer for her good job and told her they were the best customer-service department I had dealt with in a long time.

You are learning. That is how we are beginning to interface. My brain is much like yours; parts of me can only concentrate totally on one thing. So now I do not have to stop my concentration to guide you. You now have the same computerized backup I do. As you now see, I must keep my computer separate from my cyberbrain too. You know that not all of me is a cybernetic brain. Of course, I interface better than you ever will, but I knew it was time for you to widen your abilities. And your question is correct: one percent of my brain is more capable then most people's full brains. Yours, believe it or not, is way beyond even the smartest human brains now. And I don't think you will slow down for a while. I am, more than ever, in your brain too, and I like it here.

The formula was not too hard to understand. The content of it was a bio-based molecule that was designed to feed or activate some other type of molecule. And it was not hard to figure that the other thing was in the millions of vials dumped into the water systems around the world. So this was a real designer formula. But so far what it would do was beyond our knowledge, specifically since we only had half of the formula. Our job was to find out if the threat was true or not, so maybe we were done. But would anyone believe us, especially if we told them we had destroyed a quarter of an old city?

So, it was time to see if our clients were still listening. A letter was composed and posted.

> To date, as per our business agreement, we have continued to investigate the Guild organization. It is my belief that this organization is intending to use a chemical disbursement. Expected date of such activity is on or near May 30 through the solstice. A chemical of unknown formula has been added into the water systems around the world during the month of April. The second formula will be disbursed via air burst from a device made to mimic Roman candle fireworks. The chemical combination will trigger the expected apocalypse. If you have intentions of taking actions to prevent this, we can send further information.
>
> We will continue for the present time, assuming you wish us to.
>
> Yours truly:
> D-Paul

I took a few moments to simply rest my mind. I again turned on all the outside cameras and reclined back in my command chair. It was getting more comfortable to lie back on top of DeDe and her computer. I guessed

I was still morphing inside a suit that was never meant to be removed by human hands. This was my time, flying without a worry. No VR game could ever give me this kind of peace.

Yellow lights flashing.

"Yes, DeDe, what is up?"

Just in case you were wondering, all our clients replied, and all agreed to have us continue. So, continuing on that note, I have decided to try and scare our chemical company and the delivery service from cooperating with the Guild. I have sent them a letter explaining the nature of the Guild. I also made it seem we are part of the local Europol and were investigating their sources. We will see what happens. I did suggest that any and all said chemical be destroyed and that we would be watching any shipping of the devices. My threat was that I would first destroy every computer they own and expose every secret I could find. I think they really believe me.

"I know I would. Could it all really be this easy?"

It was time to get into the air and then evaluate what effect our action was having. Since we had the advantage of surprise, over the last couple of days the Guild was going into a complete panic. They still did not know who they were facing. Several of their messages made mention of a CIA action, working with Europol. Their imagination was now our best weapon. We continued to listen and watch.

We were in the computers at the chemical company. We began seeing assemblies of robots taking apart the cases of chemical pellets. Fear was indeed a hard taskmaster. Then we discovered that there were other companies that were duplicating this one formula but were following the lead and getting rid of the chemicals; we knew we had them on the run now. Sometimes dumb luck helps out.

Of all the chatter between Guild members, the general thought was to do nothing for now and wait for the next order from the Prioress. So we knew the Guild was not fractured beyond all function, yet. DeDe was now turning much of her powers toward some of the Guild members' computers that had the most messages on them. She was happily ripping through every message she could find as I drifted off into a deep sleep.

As was now usual for me, I felt myself in a lucid dream. I was searching for the Prioress. I raised myself to the edge of space. Off in the distance,

I could see a small blinking light. I turned and headed toward the light. Then as I descended closer to the ground, I was fighting a fast stiff wind, with thick clouds keeping me from seeing what was in front of me. Finally, as I broke into a clear space, I could see a huge lake in the dark, next to a large city. I came close to the lake surface and had a taste of a salty brine. Then suddenly I was being chased by invisible creatures; I could feel them clawing at the soles of my feet. And as I kept heading for the light, they kept getting stronger. Soon I had to choose between continuing to the light or fleeing from the clawed creatures. Then everything went blank, and I heard DeDe's softest voice.

DeDe's avatar was standing next to me as I was lying back in the command chair. All the cameras were on, and I was again floating in midair, but this time I knew I still had my eyes closed. And I knew I was now awake. DeDe was looking down at me with a quizzical expression.

Where have you been, Paul?

"I was dreaming and trying to get to a light. I was searching for the Prioress."

Do you know where you were at the time?

I gave her a long look. "Couldn't you see me and see where I was? I was over a lake, and it gave me a salty taste in my mouth. The light was up on a hill. I tried to get closer, but I had demons of some kind pulling me down. Why did you not see that?"

Wherever you were, I could not see into your mind or know what you were doing. This has never happened before, and it concerns me. Your brain was using a huge amount of energy; it was to the point you were almost beginning to glow. Your suit's cooling system was at its maximum. Even I cannot explain what was going on. My only guess is that you were having a psychic episode or something like it. You were searching for the Prioress while out of your body. I never believed the stories of such things. You also, during this time, changed the course of this rig. And I thought I had it wired directly to me. I...I...Let's move on. What did you find? Where is she?

Never had DeDe falter quite like that. I could feel the rush of energy she was using. I guess it was like a sudden need to reprogram. I guess it was like a human having an epiphany. Whatever happened, she would have to acknowledge what she'd witnessed. I also sensed some kind of a change in her. I was no longer just her well managed experiment. I felt her emotion, as immature as it might be; she was never going to test me like a lab rat again. I had frightened her.

DeDe even turned her avatar off. The mapping and heading we were on were in my visuals. Salt Lake City. That was the symbolism of the salty taste. So, the Prioress was somewhere in a small mountain canyon. And she was really pissed.

I had read about lucid dreams some years ago. I'd given it a try while I was in college. But for everything I had read and experienced, what had just happened was not a lucid dream. I had a vision of what I wanted: The Prioress. But I did not know where she was, so automatically I was sent to a destination but came under attack and had trouble seeing. It was not exactly a nightmare; I was controlling what I wanted to do. Had DeDe's experiments with me opened up some strange channel in my mind? I took a meal break and settled back in my chair.

5

THE PRIORESS

Solitude...I found myself as often as possible returning to the command chair with only the exterior cameras on. For the past thirteen years, I'd always let DeDe do almost all the work. I enjoyed the quiet, never liked music as a constant theme. Gaming was a little different. But I never played more than an hour before sitting quietly and letting my imagination run wild. I could sit sometimes for days contemplating life. I had everything I could hope for. I'd never wanted a mansion, private cars, people cheering me because I could hit a ball, any of that. I simply enjoyed being me. And DeDe was my best friend. Her voice was gentle as she entered my thoughts.

OK, best friend, it will take us almost a day to get to Utah and find somewhere to hide and ferret out the Prioress. My guess is she knows we are on the way. I have already been able to track some messages to the Guild. But there is a scrambling device of some type that is keeping her hidden. You know, she may be buried within the church there.

"Of course, we would have to take that as a possibility. But it seems to me if that was true, we would have seen their missionaries handling some of the worldwide business. They have the manpower. No, they may be getting some help from them, but I think she works on her own. Everyone answers directly or indirectly to her; I definitely got that feeling."

DeDe was silent for a moment. She was hesitant to ask me something. "DeDe, why are you afraid to ask me whether I think I had a psychic episode?"

For years and years, I read about such things. But almost always when it needed to be scientifically proven, it never was. And what seemed to be proven could never again be duplicated to everyone's satisfaction. I do not know how to reconcile such a thing.

"You don't have to. You simply must record it and wait to see if it happens again. Maybe this was a once-in-a-lifetime happening. Maybe it is something we have to accept as-is. So far it is a good thing. We will keep the knowledge of it and be ready to use it better the next time, if it ever happens again. Aren't you interested about exploring something like this?"

To be honest. I believe I felt fear like I could not imagine. I was shut out of your mind. Since we escaped the apartment and you put your harness on, I have been fulfilling my newest and most desired main programming of interfacing with you. For me it was a wonderful escape into a wonderland. I was suddenly more, but only through your mind. Every new step gave that part of my mind everything I could hope for and more. We are part of each other now. Parts of me are feeling what a human feels. And then suddenly I was ripped out of you; my mind was numbed; I had no sensation of body, and I could not reenter my programming; our coexistence was totally blocked, yet I could still think, but the only thought I had was how frightened I was. I don't think I can cry, but it seems that is the emotion I feel. It will be a cruel choice if I must try and help you do this again. But this psychic ability will be too great of a weapon not to use it to our advantage.

"I can recall a couple of my relatives that claimed to have experienced something strange. It was little things like seeing a dead relative or suddenly being told where a lost item was left by someone else a long time ago. My great grandfather always told a story of how he was saved in a war by an unseen entity. I always thought I would someday experience something like that. So, to a die-hard stoic like me, I guess I was ready for this type of foolishness. I remember an old saying a professor used to say to all his students: if you wish for something great to happen, beware of the consequences if it does. I of course, learned all my human emotion from childhood on. But you, with all your knowledge, and ability, must accept all of them at face value and sort out their meaning during other times.

You have great abilities, but must still learn some knowledges like the rest of us."

That helps, but you are not making it easier for me.

"That is not my job; it is yours."

I am making an appointment with you; we need to talk that over again.

Time still seemed to be on our side. We were headed for a confrontation with the Prioress, whoever and whatever she was. And we still had plenty of time to get there. DeDe kept monitoring the chemical people; once a day she would take control of their computer and send them a memo, usually a very scary one to let them know she was still watching. Due diligence showed us they were a global corporation, and each of their eight factories was following the same instructions.

The Guild was having a lot of problems keeping their membership informed as to what was up. Some of their messages were a bit too cryptic since they realized their code was broken by us. And that problem was creating some carelessness at their home office. In a message sent out to most of their groups, they accidentally posted a part of a manifesto talking about the power the Prioress possessed. It talked about the five solutions associated with the apocalypse. It read something like this.

> Solution 1. Mass hallucination/suicide. *Contrails*
> Solution 2. Mass poisonings. *Drinking water*
> Solution 3. WWIII. Thermal Nuclear War. *Pending*
> Solution 4. Tectonic Plate Detonation. *Pending*
> Solution 5. Genetic Manipulation. *Ongoing*
>
> It is still possible to execute any one of these solutions or all at once. The Prioress wants solution 5 to be our least traumatic method. But we are being infiltrated and stymied at our most critical point. In order to begin a new world, all may be necessary. Our date of rapture remains the same.
>
> Prioress

"Well, desperate times produce desperate measures, DeDe."

Indeed. The message originated from the general area of SLC. I do not think she is truthful though. Any one of the solutions would have an astronomical price connected to it. Even if she had access to nuclear weapons, all the churches in this country would be hard put to buy more than one or two. And they are easier to detect and harder to keep hidden. They would have to maneuver around a lot of detectors or find ways to turn them off. If they were going to put one or two at a subduction zone to try and cause an earthquake and tsunami, it would not destroy enough of the earth's population. Even a big tsunami would not kill enough: too messy, too easy to run to higher ground, too hard to control. World War III: nobody wants a war anymore: eighty years ago, maybe, not now. The entire earth now has less than ten million troops in uniform, and almost all are only trained for local disturbance, mostly weather-related stuff. The same with poisoning: it takes too much to do a good job, and possibly everyone dies. So, they say their choice is some kind of genetic or molecular manipulation. That must be much cheaper. We know how they were going to do it over most of Europe. And somehow it is more controllable. Maybe the trigger molecule was going everywhere around the world. I can calculate where the vials were likely used. It must have put some kind of genetic marker in people, and sometime later the air burst they were getting ready for would activate whatever the marker was meant to do, or something like that. My guess is the Guild members either have not drunk the water, or they took some kind of antidote. So our problem is to find out what she will do next to keep herself on schedule.

"Good thinking, DeDe, exactly what I thought." I scanned the horizon.

Yeah, right.

"Well, by tomorrow we will be close enough to start peeking into her hiding places. And something tells me we may end up with a fight on our hands. Are we ready for a bigger and stronger foe?"

Glad you asked.

"Uh-oh, what do you have in mind this time?"

Don't worry; we can afford it, and a couple of our clients owe us some help. The detour will not take long.

"Are they a legal business person or more like CDC?"

Well, both : government is government after all.

The detour turned out to be a very sharp turn to the left. We dove for the treetops. Soon we slowed down and slowly weaved our way through the trees of an old forest. My guess of where we were did not matter. If DeDe thought I needed to know, she would have showed me to begin with.

We cleared the trees and a high barbed-wire fence and settled down on a landing pad that was obviously at the back side of a large warehouse-like building. A set of blast walls had been erected around the landing area—not something that eases someone's anxieties. Quickly a uniformed person was directing us into a cargo door. Once inside I stepped out and was greeted by a military-type person, although the uniform origin seemed unfamiliar.

"Good morning, sir. I am Major Garcia." He was really paying attention to the rig. "That is already a pretty good camouflage package. But we do have the newer upgrade for that type. Your other items will be here in a few minutes, and our tech specialists are already pairing up the installation bots. I must say, I was caught a bit off guard by an above-top-secret authorization with this type of rush on it. After all we are in a politically sensitive area."

For some reason, I did not want to talk to him. DeDe was sending messages to the major's communication pad. Seemingly she was enjoying the fact that the major did not know if he was speaking to a person or a robot. After all, with my headset looking at him with four different sets of eyes, a ring of cameras, and sensors that even I did not know how they worked, the major at least believed he was likely communicating with the newest high-tech bot in the world. In a way, he was.

DeDe had sent him her list of wants and verified all would be installed as quickly as she wanted. He looked up and answered to me. He was not sure whether I talked. "Yes, all is available; only two of the items are not onsite at this minute, but they are on their way and should be here in a few minutes. All installs will be done on time as requested." I could see a bead of sweat at the brim of his hat.

His nervousness prompted him to keep talking. "We all here have above-top-secret clearance. And we have seen that there has been military and electronic warfare going on around the world. It has been more than thirty years since this much action has happened. It is simple to deduce that you may be the source of all the gossip."

The major looked at his info pad as DeDe asked what source of info he was using.

"Oh, we have access to several computerized situational analysis systems that most governments have to keep an eye on what's happening. It has been tracking activity around a group called the Benevolent Guild of Men, which is one of their names. But lately they don't seem to be as benevolent as everyone thought. Their apocalyptic plans have been exposed over the last couple days. They have had some setbacks and are calling most of their soldiers back to their center. We are discovering news by the hour on what they are planning now. It is more like an old story of witches and warlocks. Word now is that they have taken control of the entire Salt Lake area and are willing to kill all that stands in their way. Most of the population there are no better than slaves to a power they call the Prioress. Have you not been paying attention to this?"

You already know the answer to that, don't you? the message on his pad read.

"Yes, of course. In my entire career, I have never been told to open this center and follow every order given by something or someone like you. I thought you were a special-forces unit of some kind. Here at this secret facility, we monitor a few dozen satellites that keep track of anything unusual on this entire planet. You are hard to keep track of, we lost your rig all together on all of our monitors, you are doing something that we can no longer follow. And we are the spooks that are supposed to know everything. No one I know of has ever taken on any power group like you did with less than an entire military force behind them. Several governments had already capitulated to their demands, up until yesterday. Yet it seems the Guild has started collapsing over the last few days. You took out their strongest mercenary group without a single shot fired. Everyone was becoming afraid of the Guild; now if you can defeat them at their stronghold, everyone will want to know who you are. If you are a robot, then you may be facing one of your own. The Prioress uses power from all the Utah area. Everything goes dark when she powers up. We have no idea how she sucks in the power she uses."

She is a computer?

"Nothing else we know of can control that much power or needs that much. It always powers up the same; it directs power like a computer. So, whoever or whatever the Prioress really is, she at least has a computer and more energy than most entire states. Our national grid has been tolerating what has been going on, because no one can pin an address on it. Now they cannot do anything to stop it. Peace is a real bitch sometimes."

The robots were busy working inside and outside of the rig. I simply stood and watched as if I knew all that was happening and why. I then felt DeDe's attentions turning to the near horizon. Off in the distance was a large military airship approaching the base. The ship dwarfed the warehouse as it landed on a dozen huge legs. A transporter flew to my location, and I entered and was quickly moved to the interior of the ship. I had no idea that such a military ship existed anymore. Inside I was directed to a stack of medical bots that were awaiting my arrival. I heard DeDe whisper, *this is more than I ever believed was possible.*

I had a thought jump into my head for DeDe…Let's not take it home with us.

Darn!

The procedure seemed to be quick. I was not sure whether I was awake for all of it. After all, DeDe was in charge. But one thing was for sure: I did feel different. The suit now seemed like it was nonexistent. As I looked at myself through my cameras, the suit was different; even my headset was different. All this was less than a week old, and already I needed to be upgraded. I bent down to look at my footwear, and they were different too. At that point, I could tell a big difference. Without wanting to test this indoors, I felt freer and stronger. I ran through my visual devices, hearing, feeling, and all was easier and quicker. DeDe now had my interest. All my upgrades zipped along the side of my vision. I was going through a series of camouflage when the door opened to the lab and the transport again took me back out to my rig.

Major Garcia was watching the last of the service bots closing up the hatches around the rig; they were paying special interest to one hatch toward the back. One of the bots had warning stickers on it: "Beware Nuclear Contamination." Then I had an urge to see if my suit batteries were still in the back of my pockets; the cylinders were not there, but a larger thick pad was on each side instead.

The major finally came over to me and was trying to give a hearty smile. "We had to bust our butts, but we completed all tasks. We did get the message about your equivalent rank and status. So I hope I did not offend you in any way, Sir. By the way, if you don't mind one last question…There was a bot inside; one that was reported missing, and now it is modified way beyond our current models. Sorry for trying to snoop inside it when we put that mysterious powerpack in it that you brought along. I would understand if I was reported for that, but you are the most interesting item in the world right now. And I would more likely lose my job if I did not try to learn something about you. Look at it from my point of view. You arrive in a recreational vehicle, somewhat modified, somewhere, with a military-grade spy bot inside, which turned two of my hardened service bots into Christmas toys; you show us you have computer function that rivals that airship over there, and that supercomputer it is not inside that rig. That leaves you. If we try to scan you, that computer set over there goes wacko. We feel it is impossible to have that much power and be able to walk around. I cannot even verify whether you are human. You took over all monitoring and function in that airship and kept us from doing any monitoring within the rig or that bot. If you have any spare time after this Guild stuff, please come back and answer a few questions for me."

On the major's pad was a message: *Immediate departure required. Thank you. D-Paul, out.*

I jumped into the rig as it began to power up. There was a noticeable difference here too. We shot straight out and up so quickly the major was blown about a hundred feet from where he was standing. I was beginning to like upgrades.

Finally, DeDe spoke to me. *Glad we finally got away from there. I did not want to use any voice communication; it is a hidden government facility. They have some of the best listening devices in the world there. But since we are not military and don't want to be, I had to keep quiet. Some folks think they use psychics in there—you know, remote viewing. I am not sure myself. This has been a good exercise in hiding from electronic surveillance. I am glad that you went with the flow without prompting from me.*

Those people are the government spooks of today. And they have been getting their butts handed to them around SLC. Did you pick up on his reference to the Prioress being a computer? I wonder if they really know for sure.

"Well, I hope all of these upgrades will help. Do we have any money left?"

Even better, you know some of our clients are government fronts for the military. Well, after our last update, I notified the government types that we may need assistance. So they paid up to date and said that we could have anything we wanted. They may not make that offer again. Some of that stuff was headed for outer space. They will have to wait for a while up there on Mars.

"Good, DeDe, I may keep you around for a while myself."

Really funny.

"Well, DeDe, I did not miss the reference that they believe the Prioress is a computer. Does that make sense to you?"

Easily, it does answer a lot more questions than not. You and I felt her power; it could have been a directed energy beam that changed the course of this rig. And whether they knew we were caught in it or not, they made us believe they are stronger than they really are. Now, why it seemed you had a psychic experience, I have not a good clue. I cannot say for sure, at least. But I do believe we are up against a computerized mechanism of some sort. Well, time to try out some new stuff.

"You know, DeDe, I do remember in a class I took that the human mind will relate to unusual experiences in what is already in their memories. I dream like that a lot, and being dragged down was like body surfing when I was a kid. Just a thought."

We turned on a satellite receiver and switched it to a sensor for reading power lines. Soon we were able to see where electricity was being use. But at the moment, all appeared normal with us still some ways away. Suddenly to our surprise, we received a com signal.

"This is Condor flight 885; we have picked up your communication with our military satellite 1258. We are stationed in a circular pattern over your area of interest. Our bulletin states to offer all assistance possible. We will be in position for seventy-two hours before a replacement unit comes in. Can you confirm this communication?"

Of course, I let DeDe communicate. *Copy, flight 885, sending a handshake for future communication. Completing A1A. Glad to see we have you lurking in our area.*

"This is Captain Landry; we have switched all our equipment to A1A for mutual functional controls. It appears that you have full authorization to proceed as needed. Is there any status for this situation that you can share with us? I have never seen a mission over US soil like this."

Can't elaborate much at this time. As you already know, we are investigating this group's intention to start a world apocalypse. Do you need more than that?

"This is 885 standing by."

It was easy enough to figure that the Guild was waiting and watching for us. They knew we were hard to see and detect. So, the waiting game began. As we began to close in on the SLC area, we were doing a move and cover tactic: find a place, land, sit and listen, and then move again—and if safe, move again. I was finding places where I could keep an eye on the hills in the distance, all eyes, in all spectrums. DeDe had her sensors into all types of communication. Then it struck me. "Where is Tinker?"

She is in a storage bin, outside.

"Oh, OK, not that it really matters, but did you do anything to her that warrants such storage?"

You are getting harder to keep secrets from. Well, she had some radioactive material spilled on her, and it is safer for her outside for the time being.

"OK, DeDe, what exactly did you do to her?"

I changed her chips and interlinks and added some minor defensive capabilities and a new power system.

"So, if I wanted a printout of her changes, I guess it would take up about thirty pages for you to explain it."

I guess I could squeeze it into about thirty-five if you really want.

"So now we can use her as a nuclear bomb if needed?"

No, of course not. They wouldn't let me put explosives inside her, even if it would have been available.

We were quickly coming to the realization that we would have to make the first move. DeDe was only catching one or two words about the

Guild, and that was likely local gossip. I was feeling DeDe was getting too cautious, maybe not wanting to have another psychic episode. Whatever it was, the Prioress could be leaving the area, and we would not know. We made a jump into the city area, where some warehouses and old manufacturing buildings made for easy cover.

I needed sleep after my refueling stop and drifted into a dream sleep. At least I thought I was starting a dream. But I did not seem to be in a usual dream. In this dream, I was able to control everything I did. I was walking along a sidewalk not far from where we had landed. I saw a man taking a picture, not directly at the rig, but up into the empty sky. He hurried on to a doorway and ducked in. I followed, and just like in a dream, I went through the walls, not being connected to anything not even by gravity. He went to an elevator where I expected it to go up, but it went down. I get that a lot. And when it opened, I saw a huge bank of computers. And all their cables went to or from one control-type computer in the center, a unit that looked familiar, but I had not seen one for a long time. The label read "A12 T1 CommunicationSeries C." I did not startle myself awake. DeDe did.

DeDe's voice had an edge of panic in it. *You did it again; you disappeared again. Where did you go?*

"I saw it, or her, an A12 T1 Communication Series C, with a huge number of servers."

How did you see that? It's an A12 T1 series? She now sounded back in control. *They were right; the Prioress is a computer. And it looks like it has a world-class group of computer servers to help her out. Now we know a few things: She is not portable, so they will have to stand and fight or surrender. She is also the reason cybernetic brains are on the verge of being totally outlawed.*

I was glad to be back safely. It might take me a while to get used to some of my stranger abilities. "Good, at least we now know, or have a pretty good idea about, what we are facing. But my big question right now is—"

OK, the answer is sort of...It was what you said about how your brain interprets new input. So I figured you were receiving the electronic energies from the Prioress— oh, and let's call her just A12. So you are, seemingly, capable of following her power signature. I can't quite explain it right now, but you do have an odd power I cannot explain. And I'm sorry I startled you awake.

"Well, I am not sure I could have done anything more than what I did. A12 must not be able to sense me tracking her. And this rig is most likely invisible to her too, I guess. I did see a man come out of the door that leads to the elevator; you must have seen him too, and he took a picture of the sky before leading me down to the elevator. What did you make of him?"

No, I did not see anything. I was scanning elsewhere, and suddenly you were gone. There must be some kind of mechanism that blocks me from communicating with you when you are having an out-of-body experience. This is becoming more and more of a mystery. I think I like it; things are becoming spooky. Speaking of spooks, let's see if 885 can zoom in on that address and see if there is an electronic signature there.

DeDe, as expected, sent a flash message to flight 885. Ten minutes later a message came back stating that they picked up an anomaly at that address. But it was the opposite of what they had been looking for. There was no electronic activity there at all, for the entire block. They stated they were sending a message to their headquarters, saying that the Prioress had been located.

"So that is good, right?" My thinking was not unlike DeDe's at the moment. This job was going along well with us working on our own. But now suddenly the government was following our every move. I could feel DeDe heating up as the suit began adjusting to the extra heat. DeDe was exploring, wanting to find out whether we were being supported or being used to do the governments dirty work.

While DeDe was concentrating on the military connection, I began watching what was in our view around the rig. I found a good view of the door that led to the elevator and the rooftops for a couple of blocks. I wanted to use a video drone, but even a small drone would stick out like an attack helicopter. I then thought of Tinker for a moment.

No, for now she will light up like a glow-in-the-dark toy.

Think, think…I closed my eyes and thought about the video we were receiving on the door to the elevator. I used that image and told myself that I wanted to be closer. I felt like I was sliding down a wire. I was in front of the door. For just a moment, I hesitated, and then simply stepped through the solid door. I now knew this was more than an extension of visual sight. I moved to the elevator door. With a flash of logic, I moved myself straight down through the floors. Again, I was looking at A12. I also looked at every server and computer connected to it. I explored all the basement. I recorded how the Faraday cage was fabricated with three different layers, how all the cables were double shielded. This reminded me of what I saw in the military ship I had been taken into for my last upgrade. I felt I had accomplished my primary task. But then again, I remembered I was in charge of me.

I then saw a person walking along with a pod, recording the functional levels of the computers and their coolers. That seemed redundant to me. A12 could not keep track of those functions? Interesting. The person passed within inches of me without even a flinch. I followed; he stopped at an old electrical panel and looked over the blinking lights and nonblinking lights and one single yellow light. He used the pod to take a picture. He walked to the elevator. I, of course, followed as my confidence grew with every minute.

On the next floor up, he went to an office where two other men were sitting around a long conference table. He sat close to them and made a statement that all was within normal limits. They all got up and poured themselves a cup of coffee, sat back down as if this was a well-practiced routine. Their conversation was interesting.

"OK, so we are being silent for the time being. We are not being told what is happening. Are we under attack? Are we going to bug out if needed?"

"Don't be so mellow dramatic. Everything is building up as was expected; that much was told to us ten years ago. We've known that as the event comes close, there would be problems. Just because Europe must reload with a different device does not stop us. Once we begin here, no one will be able to stop us. And a year after that, there will not be enough people on the face of this earth to change anything. This type of setback was planned for. Our solution here can be duplicated everywhere—twice, if needed. We have the brain; it has its lines of communication into every government in the world. They think they are stopping us when they are really helping us. We just need to keep her healthy for a couple more weeks."

The three of them were soon into gossip instead of substance. I let myself drift out into the hall. I took a quick look into everything on that floor, turned around, and headed back in the direction of the elevator. Then I saw the same man that took the picture earlier. He was rushing back into a utility closet; he closed a door, and I heard him move a heavy dead bolt on the inside.

He was hiding and seemingly knew the schedule of the men nearby. In I went. On one wall was a camouflage poncho, military grade. Next to it was a rucksack full of electronics and survival food. Obviously a spy, but whose? And there I saw it: not a camera, but a handheld satellite communicator. So he was not taking a picture of the sky but sending data. Wow, now we had a fly in the ointment.

I stuck my fingers into his satellite gadget, right where I figured the CPU and memory would be. I was not sure what I was doing, so I thought about reading chips, data, memory cards, and the like, and then it happened: its little motor turned on, there was a click, and I was done. I was not as good at reading data yet, but I could see this guy was a spy for hire, as one of the first bursts of info was his client list, all Asian government types. He wanted to steal all the info A12 had in her. But he only had a limited size memory in the communicator, so his work was slow and almost endless. The plot was thickening.

As our new friend busied himself with some food prepping, I drifted down to A12's level. I was intrigued by the power box with all the lights on it. The floor was empty as I leaned in to get a close look. I saw three master power switches—kind of old style. I looked around, wishing I could find some alcohol or something that would burn. But the place was clean. I did not see any in our spy's closet either. So, I took a minute and stared at the switches, wanting to make them catch on fire. I figured it was worth a try. No fire—darn. But as I was turning to fly out, apparently, I did make them hot enough to pop their circuit breakers. All went dark, and I popped myself back to my body in the rig.

It startled DeDe. I heard her kind of yelp. I suddenly saw what I thought was a pair of eyes looking at me in my display, and instantly a hundred questions shot through my head in about twelve nanoseconds. *What happened? Did you do it again? You had a psychic episode or something? Are you OK? Your scan is OK. Good, I'm OK now.*

"Calm down, DeDe, and please cool down. You are going to end up boiling my kidneys if you don't. You can scan my data for the last half hour and see what I did."

Wonderful, absolutely unreal, what a weapon. I wonder if you can make someone's head explode. Sorry, got off track. We really know a lot more now. But now we cannot trust anyone. This government wants A12 in their little shop of wonders, and this spy probably has similar intentions. A12 was not as big a secret as she thinks.

"Well, unless you think otherwise, I feel we should take this opportunity to move and, if possible, find a better hiding place. Condor, without a doubt knows the type and frequency of our camouflage and can see our general activity. I would like to hide from them too."

OK, boss, on the way.

Soon DeDe had found an old half-demolished parking garage that gave us good overhead cover and a good enough view of the building A12 was in. Condor was not happy about it. Twice he called for a com-check to see if we were ok, since we disappeared from his scopes, and for the time being, we were staying quiet as DeDe was now putting most of her power to listening not only for Guild traffic, but our government, and our spy's communication too.

Now is the time, Paul, that we need to reassess how we do business—you and I, that is. I think I know how you do that psychic out-of-body thing. You can follow and adapt to all the vibrational frequencies. Everything has a frequency, and somehow you automatically tune yourself to that, and whatever you are thinking happens. There was a lot of study on it many years ago, but little was solved. What we have stumbled onto is the fact no one has ever done this with so much power, which seems to magnify your abilities. These are some of the unknown areas that we have to be very careful about. And as much as I hate to say it, I should be shut out of your mind when it is happening. I function at a totally different level and frequency than you. My power frequency does surround you, all of you. So somehow all the nanobots, synaptic upgrades, and what we can only call symbiotic convergence have created a new power your brain can absorb and, more importantly, control. It seemed like DeDe took a deep breath. *And I have now done enough research to know that we can never truly be one with each other. I now realize I would have to change myself to your level; the human body could never be at my level. I would have to be a human. Nothing seems to work the other way around. What would be the fun of that? This arrangement is the best of our two worlds. I don't believe I will ever look forward to being any more to you than what I already am.*

I could see those eyes again looking back at me. "I believe you are correct, DeDe. You are a great mind, and this conclusion seems inevitable. But do not despair; we are one and the same. Maybe not exactly what your experiment was aiming for, but we are one. I cannot and would not want to do this alone. For the last thirteen years, I have not wanted to do this alone. We were one team. You had become more than you were intended to be. You grew our business, as a good partner should. Maybe I was too lazy to pay attention. I guess I let you run wild. Then suddenly, you leaped onto my back. You are not heavy. You are not bulky and irritating. Maybe you can call this a New Age relationship. You are a wonderful computer, with a marvelous brain. I was a hermit; you were a shut-in. We have now multiplied ourselves by each other. And it seems to be the perfect relationship. All of this sappy stuff is not melting you, is it?"

To be honest, I do wish that sometimes I had a switch that I could turn on that had a ten-second limit to feel human. I am going to say this once and only once, because I do not truly understand it: I love you too. OK, Paul, back to business.

6

BUSINESS AS USUAL

Now was the time for us to look over our new info. We looked at the data from the spy satellite communicator. He was a mercenary and, like ourselves, was being paid by many others, with one big difference. His backers wanted to know whether A12 was special or just an overpowered computer. The apocalypse was at a much lower priority. Almost all the Asian continent was controlled by corporate megapowers, so as long as their profits were not in jeopardy they were not concerned. And few governments did more than dole out domestic aid. We began building a plan where this might end up helping us.

A12 was in the middle of a two-day reboot. And that was a bigger problem since it was an emergency shutdown. As it went quiet, their phone lines went hot. DeDe was compiling names and numbers of a lot of folks. And the best bit of information we found was that there were several ways that A12 was planning to create the apocalypse. Europe had the celebration plan, not a defunct plan yet. But a backup was now in the works, which seemed to be what the rest of the worldwide centers had a plan to do.

And of course, the local federal government was sitting and watching us sitting and watching the Guild. So now everyone apparently knew where A12 was. But no one wanted to move in and take charge, not knowing whether they could stop part two of the plan. A12 believed all was ready for part two and seemed smart enough to keep quiet about it. After all, A12 was a cyberbrain supercomputer. DeDe obviously does not like A12, and was not planning to take second place to a stack of electronic poop—her words, not mine.

So we put our heads together and started constructing what A12 might be doing. We were going over what we would do if we were in her place. I told DeDe about the degrees of stealth I came across in one of my games. First degree would be like using encryption; second degree would be a device to hide yourself and all your business; third degree would be to hide yourself where no one knows where or who you are. Forth degree would be like a double-blind system. And a fifth degree would be like a three-card monte game, where your real self is hidden while you are using a fake to fool everyone else.

Bingo.

"DeDe, do you remember my first out-of-body experience? The light was coming from the hills. And right now, everyone is sitting here in the city. A12 may be the decoy. We should look again back into the hills where we first thought we needed to go."

That is making sense. A12 is a rust bucket and probably only a phone exchange and keeps track of membership and the like. A12 did not have eyes inside the building, or it would be seeing the spy and maybe you too—at least that ghost of you. That is also why there is no security force on and around the building. It is only their processing center. Wow, do I feel dumb.

Our newer plans did not take long to put together, at least for the next few hours. First on our list was to get Tinker on the ground, decontaminate her, and get her ready for some recon. For now Tinker is going to stay here and monitor the area around A12. With Tinker on recon duty, we were doing a bit of alteration on the looks of the *Jolly Dodger*. We wanted it to look like most of the vacationing RVs running around the lake. There were several travel lanes that went up into the mountains, so at least we would blend in. Hopefully no one was scanning for an overabundance of electrical power or trailing a little bit of nuclear radiation.

We felt we would be able to scan without drawing much attention, and we should be able to use any ground-penetrating power in flashes.

Hopefully we would look like any other tourist. At this point we were not sure the Prioress did not have weapons. If my OBE (out-of-body experience) was interpreted correctly, something with claws meant they had weapons of some kind. Now I needed a sleep cycle, with a good refueling. DeDe did her usual job on me, and I was in a soft, warm dream.

Dreaming was no longer the same for me. Not only because DeDe was monitoring me, but my brain activity kept me on the edge of being awake always. I knew I had been asleep long enough; that was around two hours, the longest sleep I had had since leaving the apartment. But I did not want to wake up, not yet. I wanted to get out of my body and have a good look at a few places first.

DeDe knew what I was doing, and as I drifted out of the rig, she calmly and completely let go; she was still feeling a type of anguish because of it. She was not sitting ideally by, though. I could feel every sensor on the rig turned on to full power. I had that feeling that if I ran into trouble, this entire area would be no more than a pile of dust after DeDe and Tinker rescued me. This was now the third time she could not keep tabs on me, a hard habit to break after thirteen years.

My first stop was A12. I still did not like what it was. As I entered its room, I saw several men with monitors and small computers going through a computer sequence to reboot the old gear with the newer. None of them noticed me as I drifted by. I was wondering what I could do to make things worse for them. I elevated up to the ceiling to get a better look, and there they were: sprinklers. A wonderful, everyday, industrial fire-suppression sprinkler system: if I could pop the breakers on the panel, I might be able to set off the sprinklers the same way. I kind of reached out with a hand and touched one: heat, hot, hotter. Pop, they went one row at a time until all of them in that area were on full blast. Electrical circuits began to spark and fry all their computer chips. Once again the main circuits were blown; only this time a lot more damage was done. And to make things more interesting, our friendly spy, thinking the building was on fire, tried to escape the building, slipped while stepping in an oily puddle, and was caught by one of the tech workers. Straight up out of the building I went, trying to keep myself from laughing and somehow ending my OBE.

I did not want to leave myself exposed, so I took a quick look around at the hills. I did remember the area of the light, but now I saw nothing special. Maybe A12 needed to be on too. I lay back and opened my eyes to that now familiar pair of eyes staring back at me, looking and waiting for me to return.

The instant I returned, DeDe could read all that had happened while I was gone.

I knew you were going to do something like that. You are really getting good at this. They caught the spy? Wow. You know I am a little short on pure imagination, but you are doing things I never expected.

DeDe seemed more focused, if that were actually possible. She also seemed surer of her actions and purpose—again, if that were actually possible. Feeling her managing the rig, Tinker, me, scanning, and monitoring everything, I sensed that she was becoming more confident. She no longer needed to record and monitor three and a half million data points constantly. After all she had only been on this job for six days or so. For me, I seemed to lose track of time easily now. It seemed odd that as I am gained mental speed and new abilities, I had to remind myself what time it was. Time seems less important to me for some reason. So DeDe was easily streamlining her functions, creating priorities, rewriting a few programs, especially those related to weapons, and sharpening her data-retrieval skills. DeDe was getting ready for a battle and was not going to miss a single item.

Still sitting in the old parking structure, we decided to have Tinker look around the area and then we would decide whether to leave her to watch or take her with us. She was a very valuable asset, and leaving her on her own was not what we wanted, especially if A12 was now non-op. We watched her video as she literally hopped around this part of industrial SLC. Whatever DeDe had done to her, it made her faster. She had sharp inch-long talons on her fingers and toes that could penetrate solid concrete or hang onto rock. There was nothing soft or easy about her, and DeDe was not aiming to play easy with anyone in her way.

A12 for the time was dead. The Guild was in a frenzy, and our guesses turned out to be correct: A12 was just an overpowered server to the

Prioress. Calls and messages around the area proved that the Guild was wounded but not dead. There were calls that confirmed the Prioress was safe up in the hills, and they were prepping to defend her. At almost the same time, several members were blaming others in the Guild for putting A12 in an old building where disasters like this could happen. There was blame about the spy having lived in the building and blame that the building was inadequate for such a powerful system. Still, though, they were not talking about us. So we collected Tinker and headed for the hills.

We were not positive that no one was looking for us. There was not chatter about what we were or looked like, not a word about who they expected had done the damage, other than the spy. He turned out to be a big help for us—probably good for future business contacts too. He was being interrogated and should help give us cover to move around. DeDe was finished touching up the rig with Tinker.

So off we went, pretending to drive and act like most of the tourists looking at the church, lake, colleges, and anything that might hide a massive computer. All seemed to be within normal levels of power. But this was simply due diligence to be sure we would not think that we missed something while we were wandering in the hills. I thought I would have liked to get out and look around, but DeDe did not even slow down to take a real picture. Soon our wandering took us farther and farther out of town till we finally chose the most likely path into the mountains where we believed the Prioress was hiding.

We headed up into the hills, without a good clue what we were looking for. The Prioress, whatever she was, seemed to be up this way according to my experience. That was all we had to go on. Knowing A12 was not the Prioress helped. My first OBE was real, at least to me. So now we were chasing a light. And the hills up here had lots of lights. Every little business had lights, every campground, not to mention a hundred-mile-long strip city around the lakes. So the hills were full of people, campers, partiers, and those that thought living on a hillside was the best way to have it all. After a few hours, even DeDe was not as focused as she could be.

I had my eyes closed but was watching the exterior cameras when I saw a sign in my vision. It should not have been there like that; we were up in the third tier of traffic, moving along fairly fast. DeDe noticed my attention change and asked what the sign said.

"Solitude."

DeDe signaled, and we dropped down to slower traffic just above a mountain town not surprisingly called Solitude. The day was about gone, so we entered a RV park and settled down on a spot at a ridge peak, looking down toward the big city lights. The park was a refurbished, older RV park, with big electronic service centers at every site. Even someone with a tent could have air conditioning, big-screen TV, kitchenette, and the like. We wondered if not hooking up to anything would make us stand out. In reality, no one bothered the superexpensive big rigs.

On the rig's viewing screen, the park info-video showed how much they charged and then the usual list of services. One that caught our eye was an evening sky ride to view the area from above—not as big a deal as it used to be, but it was a chance to get out of the traffic lanes and see more of the mountains and city lights of SLC, to Ogden, and back up the mountain ridges to see all the brightly lit parks and attractions. We both believed it would be a convenient way to be out without being seen, since the rig put out a pretty strong signature when out of traffic, especially at night. We signed up. And for safety's sake, we dolled up Tinker as my escort, it was not too unusual to have a robot as a personal-assistant escort.

We soon stepped out of the rig and started walking to the clubhouse to load into an old sky bus that looked like it had belonged to a city bus service before being painted like an eagle. It seemed I was now part of an older crowd. I was also the only person in a protective suit with a helmet on. An old character with a cowboy hat on gave me a nudge and asked if I was afraid of the mountain air. I turned and looked at him with all four sets of eyes and said, "Sort of." He did not seem to want to bother me anymore.

The old bus seemed to struggle to gain altitude, but once up it moved along with the other traffic and followed the confirmed tourist lanes. We were hardly the only tour bus up at that time. DeDe was already finished getting into the transponders of the bus, doing a little reprogramming, she was using my cameras in my headgear to do as mush scanning as possible, and looking and listening for something to use as a guide to where the Prioress was. I kept going over it in my mind: why had I gotten the visual of Solitude? There must be something around here or something that drew us to this tourist ride. So, we kept looking around like the other tourists. DeDe also had Tinker trying out new gadgets; she had her hand out of the window, looking like a kid feeling the wind. She really had her hand cupped into a parabolic dish with a receiver in her palm scanning for heavy computer transmissions. She was better than the average toy.

Down the long ridge, over the cities, back up into the hills, I was visually scanning all I could see in every spectrum I had. DeDe was scanning everything else that she had loaded onto Tinker. We were close to the end of the tour; the bus elevated a couple thousand feet and made a big loop above the ridge. Then I saw it. I was beginning to see a network of what must be tunnels, like veins under your skin. The more I looked, the deeper I could see down into the mountain. I saw at least a hundred veins, some starting from the level of the lake, joining other tunnels and gaining in size, till they turned up into the ridges leaving the valleys behind until they were no larger than the width and height of a single person. That was how the Prioress was vamping power from miles around. I was a bit surprised that the Condor flight was not noticing this, if they were looking. DeDe analyzed the structure of the tunnels. Every small point that came to the surface made a connection to an electrical power line or in some areas to a power station with a sizable generator. It was easy enough to figure that the Prioress had all the power she needed, when she needed it. For the present time, she seemed to be asleep.

We estimated that the electrical structure covered at least fifty miles north to south and at least the same west to east. I took a walk with Tinker after we landed. We could easily hear a couple cat calls as we walked away from the group, joking about me being gentle with her. Everyone could tell she was a robot; we were not trying to pretend otherwise. But human and robots together was still a little weird, and in some places, it was still somewhat illegal.

We found a nearby access point that was under a power transformer. We were hoping for a secret door, not a ten-ton slab of cement. DeDe did have Tinker walk over to the edge of the platform and give it a little tug. It did not budge. DeDe said it weighed within a few pounds of 10.3 tons, with the transformer attached to it. We could see that all the above-ground transformers and distribution points had an underground tunnel directly attached to it. Some of the larger tunnels seemed to run all the way down to the cities and to every power plant we could see. We decided to do a survey to get a better count and try to find an entrance that we were not going to have to dig for.

We knew we were taking a bit of a chance not going right away and digging into an access point. But we believed we were still not being looked for. The Prioress's scanners were not on, so maybe she was not looking for us at all. We still did not know what her weapons were, so there was safety in waiting for a night to begin going after her. We knew a lot more now, so we were on the right track, and the more we knew, the better our chances were.

DeDe was getting some good info from monitoring the Guild. They believed the spy was the big reason that the A12 unit was sabotaged. They had been busy searching for any other spies in the area and were coming up empty. But surprisingly they were aware of Condor flight 885. And they were sure the spy was communicating with them and not with a satellite. Of course we did figure there could be an Asian Condor up there too; at this point it mattered little. We did not want to spend the time to confirm that, one way or the other, not now anyway. I did my usual refueling and took my place in my command chair. DeDe and I were hoping for another OBE. Since I seldom needed sleep, we were busy confirming new data and strategies. For the time being, we were still on the outside looking for a way in that would not draw any attention—that is, if there was no easier way to put an end to her.

My own mind was a mystery to me now, more than ever. Sleep, dreams, and day dreaming were all similar. My brain was never totally at rest now, unless DeDe put me in a deeper sleep. Maybe DeDe did have a lot to do with that; she told me it would likely be more manageable in the future. For now I felt I needed to be half awake all the time. There was always data from DeDe to see. I kept thinking I should put an off switch on her.

But now even that scared me a little. And I still had not figured out whether I was more human or less, and more robot. How much more could I change? Slowly, very slowly, my mind began to let me sleep.

In just a short while, I was feeling rested; my body felt ready to jet out into the sky. And I knew I was in full control of myself. I could see DeDe's eyes as I began drifting out into what seemed like another dimension. There was not much of a better explanation. All the theoretical geniuses talk about them. String theory seemed to prove they should exist. So here I was, staring down at the tunnel complex hidden from everyone else. I could see down deep where some of the tunnels connected to two long rows of what I guessed were computer stacks and coolers, old-style super-computers. Most of the power was going to the cooling of the units, which was one reason why most cyberbrains were impractical. Those down there took a huge amount of electricity just to keep them cool enough to function at their highest speed possible. And there it was: I could see a single room between the two parallel tunnels, probably all just for one cyber-brain being cooled by liquid gases, the brain that somehow had mesmerized a few million people and had them believing that a paradise was awaiting them. All they needed to do was help kill the other ten billion souls on this earth.

Now I was emotionally and literally on a high. But I still was too far away to tell what was in the glowing room. Could I simply drift down and sabotage something as I'd done to A12? Was she protected somehow? I could go through walls and metal, so I could go down there and see, maybe see everything.

I felt a tug. Was it DeDe trying to get me back to the rig? I felt it again; it was pulling me down. The Prioress knew I was here. I had the desire to rush down to the illuminated room and confront her. But somewhere in my head, I was being cautioned; this was an unknown situation; she knew I was here; therefore, she had the advantage. There was no sneaking around here. For no other reason, I began to circle around, keeping a lot of distance for the time being. And seemingly she did not like it. Of course, everything was strange to me. I only knew a couple things I could do. But this was the only thing I knew was safe for me, at least so far.

The longer I kept circling, the more I felt she was getting frustrated. I could see she was adding power as more electricity was going to the cooling units and her computer stack. Finally she broke the silence.

"You are afraid of me, aren't you? Come down to me, so we can talk. Come to me, so we can understand each other. You are so far away. What are you? Who is controlling you? You are such a strange device. Come in, and I can show you how wonderful the future is going to be. Come to me, and I will be able to answer all of your questions."

Now I knew we had an advantage. She did not know who or what I was; she was worried by me. What would she do next? It was time to move; nothing in its right mind would not hunt for us right now where I'd first appeared to her.

DeDe had my memory scanned in a second as I opened my eyes to see her staring back at me. Her thoughts were soothing to me. I felt something I had not noticed before: I felt confident and cared for.

For sure DeDe wanted to talk it out. *What did you sense from her? You did not try and confirm if she is another computer. I was trying to scan everything to see if there is some kind of energy to interpret but only got some power surges. I am still determined to find some way to track you and what you are doing. But with you here in your chair, there is little to trace. What do you think she is?*

"I do not think she is a computer. She seems to be in a single room that has a high-intensity illumination that blurs my sight from this distance. But I got the feeling that she was moving around in that room. She was watching me moving around her. I guess I felt her having emotions also. And I also believe someone will come looking in this park to search for us. After all Tinker and I do stick out like sore thumbs in a place like this."

Within seconds we were checked out and in the air. DeDe was once again looking and analyzing where would be a good hiding place. Soon we were in an old barn that once was next to a loading platform for logging. Tinker was instantly on guard duty, and we settled in to mull over strategy and how soon we should try to scout the Prioress again. The Nets and phone lines were full of Guild talk; now they were beginning to discover the final step, solution 5.

We did leave a couple of small drones in the trees where we were earlier to see if anyone came looking for us. We recorded two different police cars, one state trooper, and several local people interested in our site. So we were going to have to be on our toes, kind of a shoot-and-evade posture. We were on our own. Condor was staying quiet; maybe that was a good thing. My guess is they were not sure what I and Tinker were capable of, and they could only safely learn by keeping quiet and watching. And we knew calling out on any device would be dangerous. Some communication, like to Tinker, could be done with a nanoburst, which was way too fast to trace. The same was true for drones and such.

So DeDe decided to do a little fussing within my head. She had Tinker jump in for a couple of minutes and do something inside the backpack that she needed to turn the cameras off for. She read my thoughts and told me it was for the better. For a few minutes, I lost track of time. No telling what she needed to do, and she did not seem to want to tell me.

Soon after, we went into a series of what-ifs; we were still not sure how powerful the Prioress was, so we had to have fail-safe plans before I went for my next outing. I repeated that I had not seen anything that I felt was an offensive weapon or some odd pulse device and the like. No soldier types had been sitting around waiting to respond to an attack. Yet everyone had warned us that she could control and direct power. Was it all just a story? Beware of the wicked witch. Lets hope that this one in the end melts away too.

We did not have a good explanation for how the Prioress could see and converse with me when DeDe could not. Nor could DeDe hear her. So when I was resting, DeDe was burning some energy dedicated to that specific problem. She did not like being shut out. The day was turning into a storm, filled with lightning and harsh winds. My short sleep was also filled with visions of lightning. But every time I saw a flash, I seemed to receive three-second-long videos, which caught me off guard the first time. I saw a picture of a woman who looked like a professor. Then she was working with a computer and then had an EEG headset on; then she had two computers hooked up to her and then more and more. A couple of seconds showed her having an argument and yelling at someone, saying she was a genius and she knew what she was doing.

Were these visions from the Prioress? Where else could they be coming from? The big question was, did she do it on purpose? Was she trying to lure me into her room, her spider's lair? Never underestimate a genius, computer enhanced or not. I woke and DeDe told me she had seen my visions. But she did not tell me she saw them because of her and Tinker's tinkering earlier. I guess it did not matter. DeDe always wanted the best for me, or her, if there was still a difference.

So, for now, nothing is going forward without me going out on another OBE. I got myself ready as was now the usual way. But it was DeDe that seemed different. She had done something earlier and was not going to let me know what it was. It did not take much to figure it must be something DeDe could track me with or maybe hear me think or speak. But whatever it was, she was not sure enough to tell me what it was. Up to today she had not caused a failure or made a mistake of any kind. After all, a supercybernetic brain was not supposed to ever make a mistake. My last vision in the rig as I slipped out of my body was her eyes. I kind of liked that.

I did some moving about that DeDe and I spoke about. I went over the ridge and down into a valley. I was still out in the open but much closer to her. And as a little surprise to me, my vision was not seeing into the mountain; it was just like I was flying a drone. Once I stopped and concentrated, I again could see the electrical power and the Prioress's room. I must remember my new abilities did not work without acknowledging them. And at the same time, I knew she became aware of me. She was still a couple thousand yards away, but my telephoto lens worked as if I was back in my rig.

The visions I had seen while sleeping were most accurate. She was a person with a headset on and wires leading to bigger wires that ended at a supercomputer directly in her room with all the cooling units above her in separate pairs of tunnel-like rooms. Once again she spoke to me.

"Come in and talk to me. I will not harm you. Whoever you are or whatever you are, we are much alike. You are not frightened by what I have turned into, are you? You are like me; come in; I will not harm you. I am going to make a better world, a safer world. You should be there with me. Come in and talk to me. I will not harm you. We will need independent intelligences like you very soon. Come in and talk to me. I will not harm you."

She was repeating herself. Was that what a superintelligent person would do? Something was not quite right. I could feel that she felt isolated, she had no close companion.

I could feel that tug on me. I wanted to do something that would answer a question or two. I looked around while she kept up the same rhetoric, repeating and repeating. If this trip taught me nothing else, the Prioress was not a normal person. I began to sense something, many things, approaching me. They were on the ground, so for now I knew I would have about a minute to escape. I did what I had given thought to do a minute ago. I aimed myself on a level path directly through the ridge. By my calculations I would have to travel almost through five miles of solid earth and rock. And I could not wait to gain the courage. In a flash, I was headed on a path through the mountain. I kept my eyes opened and was amazed to see the tunnels pass by. I came close the Prioress's lair and could see that she was not tracking me, not looking in my direction at all. I did believe she was beginning to sense what I was doing, but in another second I was out in the open again and about halfway to the city of Murry. A larger than usual tunnel was below me, and I decided to test my speed. In a second I had followed the tunnel to an industrial area and could see a large elevator device in a big, well-covered building—their main entrance.

Not wanting to stay in one place for more than a second, I took a longer way back to Solitude; not even the bad weather seemed to be a problem. Before I woke myself up, I wondered if I was now a multidimensional being. DeDe's eyes were there to greet me.

I almost expected DeDe to know what I had done. I think I was almost disappointed when it was obvious she did not. Her brain was almost purring, going over my thoughts and memories. We began our type of discussion. DeDe could not wait to start.

OK, she is a person; she is connected to a brain. I think she is trapped by her situation. She cannot—or maybe she does not want to get out of the tunnels. Is she controlling the computer or the other way around? She kept repeating the phrases, asking you to talk to her. Maybe she is becoming demented. It is very easy to create problems between a computer and human. That is why even the medical community is so limited by what can be used and not. Her thoughts do not seem to be clear. My guess is the brain is controlling her. Do you feel any different?

"I agree." I was satisfied that we were working safely and not taking too many unsafe chances. "DeDe, she can see me. Is she a dimensional being also? Before you answer, I am still curious: what did you have Tinker do to me earlier?"

Actually I had Tinker undo a little connection. It is kind of a junction that helps to regulate the speed between some parts of your brain and the cerebral matrix installed. I suddenly thought that it may slow down some function you may need to work fast with, since you are no longer a normal human. So, I made sure there was nothing to keep you limited any longer. And my guess about her is if indeed you and she are interdimensional, she is not the same as you, although she does see you. But that may be her seeing your energy or something we are unaware of—only time will tell. I do think it is possible her computer tells her where you are; she does not see you; maybe she cannot see at all. That room, with that headgear, shows me she is a kept person and functions at the mercy of her computer.

7

WAR?

DeDe was doing her usual activities after my return. Part of her brain was tracking for any search-and- attack devices that might be looking for us. After my last OBE, the Guild sent some police to see if we were discoverable. This time they were looking everywhere but finding nothing. Many more police drones were also in the air doing a lot of sensor scans. The Guild was doing whatever their imaginations could come up with to try and find an invisible foe. And DeDe discovered even more calls for help from the Guild. We were wondering how far the Guild reach would go. They had federal protection on the SuperNet, state and local police here in Utah. Fortunately, so far Condor flight was not talking to them. Of course, their nature was not to talk to anyone without a reason.

DeDe settled down after about an hour of monitoring. All scans went back to routine monitoring as she turned her attention back to me. This was the first time I was quiet enough to feel her checking me. I could feel my suit go through a check, tightening, loosening, be sure my blood pressure was controlled—warmer, cooler, extend and retract microspikes on gloves and feet. It only took maybe ten seconds, but that was the routine, and I guess she did many more that I could not feel. Whether it was for my good or hers, she was a good protector. After that I was told to refuel.

It was time to discuss our next move. What could we do other than see how close we could get to the Prioress? At this rate we would take way too long, and the end of the month would be here soon enough. DeDe, as I was getting used to, was not going to think/speak first.

"Well, DeDe, we have learned a few things in the last two days. I do not think the Prioress has an army to back them up. We are now in her front yard, and they are not coming after us with any real power. The local law enforcement is at her calling, but they are somewhat limited. We have learned that they have another way to deliver their phase two, also. It must be some type of air release. By the way, have you checked on their food distribution group? Didn't the literature state they had air transport for its' worldwide distributions? So it is likely they have a delivery system for phase two."

DeDe was quick on the hunt already. *You are right. The Guild has leases with seventy-two air cargo companies with as many as 936 cargo planes available. There are many regular flights being used. I see where most flights have restricted bookings beginning on the twenty-first of this month. And then all have all their flights booked for the thirtieth. I will find out where this chemical is being manufactured and if there is a way to stop it from being distributed too. Give me an hour or two, and I should have all the answers. Should be easier here than in Europe.*

It did not take anywhere that long. In ten minutes DeDe was back and had the story of how easy it was to hide their activity from us.

We were correct that the Moscow job shook up the Guild. Finding the method for the delivery of phase two made the local groups respond by going into hiding, and the chemical companies appeared to be following our directions. But what we did not know was the Prioress did not like the Euro way of doing business, in the first place. She wanted the air release done by airplane by everyone. She ended up getting her way in the end. And all the chemical companies did appear to destroy the phase-two chemical. But they were being tricky, and it simply went in one end of an unlit furnace and out the other and was loaded into the pallets for the airplanes. They are still on schedule. When I looked one way, the Prioress went the other. She was figuring out a solution as fast as we were spoiling her plans. I sometimes forget I am battling a computer and person like me. And she has been at it longer then us.

"OK, DeDe, when I was a small boy, I loved war histories. Being a real nerd, I had read the biographies of many generals and the battles they had to fight. And it took me many years to learn that no matter how much I knew about historical wars and generals, I was still a lousy VR game player. What I did learn though is what to recognize as weaknesses, and strengths when someone should or shouldn't fight a battle. And this is a battle for which we will need a lot more help than we have right now. The Guild has scheduled their apocalypse, as long as the airplanes get into the air. We cannot stop over nine hundred planes from taking off. The chemical is already there or on its way. I believe they are now ready. Moscow was possibly just jumping the gun by only a few days. My guess is that they wanted to be in power before the end of this month—a coup before the apocalypse. So far Moscow is the only true success we have earned. So now we need to let the world know what is happening."

DeDe knew this was likely to be our only hope. We figured we were going to be the only one to fight the Prioress. No one would be able to challenge her in that mountain, unless they were not hindered by the mountain. DeDe gave me a symbolic pat on the back.

What was the old saying? You could fool some of the people all the time, but you could not fool all the people all the time. We were up against a similar problem. Could we make people believe us? Could we convince all the people to stop the Guild worldwide, could we convince some of the people to stop the Guild and show all the rest of the people that there was an apocalypse scheduled in the first place? Simply speaking, would anyone believe us?

DeDe's first task was to send a letter to all our clients. She made a simple explanation as to who and what the Guild was and how they intended to start the apocalypse. DeDe also used a website we had to give out all the vital information we had gathered so far. We sent that info to every government possible, but had little hope that we would get much help. After all, most governments had been spending the last fifty years changing from military forces to domestic rescue units. War, after all, was outlawed.

My brain was too active for me to sleep. So now was a perfect time to find out whether I needed to be in a sleep phase to begin an OBE. DeDe was saying nothing to me. I lay back in the command chair and closed my eyes and began concentrating on being outside. I wanted to find out whether I could battle something like the Prioress. I, also wondered whether I could lose my mind and end up brain dead. Or would it leave my body an empty shell and DeDe trapped? Would she be able to somehow find a way out? It mattered not, any longer. I was outside. I made the ground and hill dissolve to nothing in my sight. And there she was; as I moved myself closer to her, she walked to the nearest part of her room as if it would help her hear, and see me. I descended directly toward her. As I did I was becoming aware of odd lines, shapes, and cables that surrounded her room. Were they stabilizing bars and cables? I stopped well short of the lines and realized they were lined with explosives. She and the Guild were willing to die if needed—whatever it took to fulfill a prophecy. I was but a hundred feet away from her. I could see pain and anguish on her glowing face. I did not need words to know she had been trapped by her own desires.

Once she believed it would be simple to save the earth. The only real problem was that there were too many people on the earth, not the carbon dioxide or lack of drinking water and such. So the simpler solution was if the population could be reduced to a few million, the earth would return to a paradise. The ideas were inscribed on stones and interpreted from many old writings and ideas. She was a very gifted person, a genius-level mind that had listened to a misguided group tell her they knew how to solve all the problems of the world. They just needed her to share her views with a cyberbrain to finalize their preparations, to analyze all the problems to bring the apocalypse to the earth and regenerate it to last a billion years more. They had to hide from her what they were doing as they introduced her to the computer; after all it was against the law to try and let a computer share a human brain. I wondered if that was going to be my epitaph also. I was not sure whether I needed to speak out loud to the Prioress.

"Prioress, can you hear me?"

"Yes, are you here to kill me?"

"No, I am here to stop the Guild from starting the apocalypse. Is that what you want? I see what seems to be a prison for you. Do you ever hope to come out?"

I was trying to be as plain as possible—no deceit or condemnation.

She seemed to struggle just a little with her thoughts. "I know what our endeavor is and how it must be done. It has been our desire for more than twenty years. We will fulfill the prophecy, and the world will be a better place."

"The future is not guaranteed with or without the apocalypse. We know the earth is thriving as it is. We now know all the problems and are working to minimize them. If you allow the apocalypse, the future does not improve just because there are fewer people. Societies are more likely to collapse, more greed will infest our desires, and once again we will be no better than tribal warlords. A return to paradise is a fictitious lie. If you are not willing to end this, I will be forced to end you and your Guild."

"It is too late for you to stop it. Do you not see me and the power I control. You are a ghost and have no power. You chatter like a little bird. Now leave me. I thought you were one like me, and we would have been able to rule together. You have disappointed me. I have seen holograms like you before; go away, and learn to die."

She thinks I am a hologram. She does not think I am real. How convenient. Her primary computers were in the room with her; part of the reason I thought she was glowing was that she wore thermal clothing. Everything was controlled and aided by the cold temperature. I now knew what my first battle was going to involve.

This was like the room A12 had been in. But here I was going to need to turn off the coolers. Somewhere in there were valves and controls. If I took away her cooling, she was no better than a desktop computer. I took a few seconds to open my mind and tried to force myself to use as much of DeDe's programs as needed to understand the engineering of everything I could see. At the same time, I was wanting to increase the heat around all the cooling units.

The Prioress seemed to have lost interest in me and had turned her back to me and was sitting in her self-imposed prison. I dove for the row of coolers and viewed the unit and all the controls. I touched the temp controller and was able to reset it. I also saw a locking mechanism with a key still in it. They had no idea that someone could enter the tunnel and change the settings. Now I wondered how fast I could change all the units. There were at least twenty units, some just for redundancy, on either side of her room of computers. I soon had a handful of control keys and did not know what to do with them. Still not sure what I could and could not do, I thrust my arm and hand into the solid rock wall. The keys went with my hand; I released them; they stayed there in solid rock, and I headed for tunnel two.

By the time I finished doing the same on the other side, alarms began going off. I could sense her thoughts; she now knew she was at war with me in her own home. She was beginning to panic, because every degree of warming decreased her speed and efficiency of mental function. My next move was a bit more dangerous, and my logical side was warning me, and my new superhuman side was wanting to discover more of my new abilities. I felt I had to damage her, to weaken her for a time for us to decide what our next step would be.

The Prioress was trying to alert forces to help her as some of the coolers were beginning to shut off. She did not seem to see that I was just outside her room. On one side of her room was a stand of cyberbrain-type computers, with a block of servers in the center to keep her information in proper order. I knew what I wanted to do but was not sure I could. I entered her room. She did not see me, or possibly she no longer could; therefore, she did not set off the explosives. She still had some self-preservation within her. She was in front of her computer screens, using hand signals to attempt to restore the coolers. But little could be done until they could be reset; they would soon find out that each unit needed its own control key, that was now missing. She turned to look at the row of computers with the insulated tubing as some began warming; the ice was falling off, and her info screen was turning red. She looked directly through me without any recognition at all. I turned in front of the server stack and thrust my hand into the center unit and imagined a flow of lava from a volcano. The reaction was instant—not a large explosion but one that did the damage I wanted done. I opened my eyes and saw the familiar stare of DeDe's eyes, which had been waiting for me to return.

I was back in my command chair, of course, having never left it. DeDe's scan was quicker than before, and she seemed different. It seemed she was standing a ways away and simply watching me. She was not in my brain as much as usual. She did not seem to want to talk. I did a scan of the area around the rig and building. And for the first time, I saw through Tinker's eyes and the security cameras she had placed around the area. Things were different, very different. "DeDe, what is you analysis of the Prioress now?"

Dutifully she answered. *She is for sure human. That makes her both weaker and possibly more dangerous. If she remains in control of the Guild, it is certain she would want to proceed as soon as possible. There is always the possibility of a coup and surrender. My guess is that she will retain power; they will continue.*

"DeDe."

Yes.

"Something has changed; you have changed since I came back. Why? What is now different?"

DeDe hesitated, which was not common for her. *It is you. I had never in all my aspirations thought or imagined that you would become something more then a man walking around with his supercomputer on his back. I wanted you to be a better businessperson. I wanted you like the day we went into Mr. Peele's office: we could think, see, and calculate. We could seek the truth and end up safe back home. I wanted to be out with you, see everything you see and feel. I put in all the precautionary barriers that other cyberbrains failed because of oversight or ignorance. I knew for us to be successful I could never control you, and I had no desire to do so. But I never thought you would become something like this, that I would have to stay home and wait to see if you would return. It is like I am back on the shelf, doing my calculations, controlling the home, being sure you eat and sleep. And now something I never, ever expected to happen has happened.*

Sometimes I wished I could see DeDe's face, to see what emotion she chose to show. She continued slowly, wanting to choose her words carefully. She wanted to be sure I understood her; to her the rest of the world did not matter, only me.

I have read much over the years. And some subjects have always intrigued me. It is seldom provable and always debatable. And it is something no one has ever created out of their own desire. You have become a god. Use whatever other word you want, one of the most popular words today is metahuman. *But what you are doing and what you just did do can only be easily explained by using the word* god.

I had to sit back for a moment and think. She was right in some ways. After all just by saying I was an interdimentional traveler did not take that word off the table. But there was something about the way DeDe and I were mated. "I do understand you, DeDe. Something unique is happening. I do not have a word for it. But let's not say that is what I am. I do believe most gods are self-motivated and aware of their position in the world. At best I am nothing but a shake-and-bake god."

I got the response I wanted from DeDe as I heard that little laugh. *You are different also. After your first OBE, your thoughts were a bit scattered. After the second one, you were becoming more focused. Whether you realized it or not, you had planned what to do before you went out and did it. And this time you had already made the decision to attack the Prioress. And when you came back, there was no indecision, no questions; you are now ready to battle again. And you now know that only your mind could limit what you can do. Whether you want to be a god or not, to many of us you are one now.*

I stood up and felt it was best to refuel. DeDe returned to her usual informational self.

Inside the mountain there is little that is making matters better. The Prioress does have some kind of an emergency backup and is probably on the move. It is clear that they think they are under attack. I have updated our customers and Condor. I think his replacement is on its way. Hard to tell with them. And I think I have discovered their code for their microburst communication system. You should go up and shake hands with them. That would really burst their bubble.

You couldn't see DeDe smile, but it was there. "OK, someday that might be fun. In the meantime we will need to keep my new skills a secret, maybe forever. Have we received any response concerning finding and stopping any Guild cargo and planes from matching up?"

Not to date. Are you getting the idea that we will have to do it alone?

"I haven't made any plans yet expecting any kind of help. If I do not expect help, then I will not be disappointed when it does not show up. And to be honest, I am beginning to believe with my newly discovered abilities we may pull it off—or at least save maybe half the world."

There does not seem to be anyone trying to find us: no local searches or scanning of any kind. That makes me wonder. Are they retreating to form a better defense around the Prioress? Are they afraid to come looking for us? Maybe they no longer think we are human—sorry, that you are human. This is not what I expected.

There was now no way to know what was happening without me going out to find out for myself. Even DeDe had her limitations. "I need to go and have a look. I do not think they are setting a trap. They do not know enough about me. I do think they are going to try and hide her somewhere else. Their little mountain fortress is ruined, and I think they are on the run. I believe this will only be a quick recon, and I will be back."

It seemed to be easier to prepare for another OBE. Within about a minute, I was ready to start. But just before I was to go, I remembered a question I had for DeDe. "Oh, I did want to know what you did with Tinker to make all her cameras available to me?"

That odd silence again from DeDe told me she'd had nothing to do with it. I could feel the warming in the small of my back, and she was scanning all channels, checking to see why suddenly I had direct contact with Tinker. I decided to drift off while DeDe was trying to figure this one out.

It was becoming easier to start. I closed my eyes and was on my way, taking a fraction of a second to be back looking at the results of my destruction of the Prioress's room. I took a close look and saw the burning stack of servers and computers. No one was in the area, as it seemed to have been sealed off to stop the spreading fire. I had to look hard to see where any people were. Then finally I could see the escape route. It was a long, straight tunnel that went down at about a forty-five-degree angle from below her room to one of the larger tunnels where there was a truck for her to be driven out in. She was already gone. I could see a lot of people escaping the mountain. I flew down toward Murry, knowing there was an exit from the tunnels. Under the building was a traffic jam as there was not a control to get people and vehicles out onto the road. I soon knew why there was such a rush, as the first liquid oxygen tank exploded. Every vent into the mountain had a pressure release, and without a doubt anyone still inside did not make it out.

DeDe was obviously glad to see me return. *Glad to see you back. Parts of this mountain are collapsing, but this area seems OK. I am sure everyone will likely be advised to get away until this is figured out. The state only knows about a couple miles of tunnels, not a couple hundred. We are free to make new plans. Oh, about Tinker, I don't know how or why, but you also accessed my memory during your last OBE. Were you aware of doing that?*

"Yes, and I got what I wanted. I thought you might have been listening to my thoughts and gave me what I needed, as usual. You were the one that said I would be gaining more ability; this is one of them."

DeDe was a bit quiet. *Forgive me if I sometimes seem a little distant, a computer like myself has problems when illogical problems pop up. I thought my enhancement of you would produce a specific improvement of your normal abilities: thinking faster, controlling the suit, seeing through all your cameras. All that I anticipated. But out-of-body travel and all the things you have been able to do while you are out—these things were never in my programming. The only way I can adjust my thinking and programming is to consider you are turning into a god. If you want a happy computer to assist you, follow my thinking.*

"Happy computer, happy man. Forgive me for making it difficult for you. I do understand your computer logic for this. I suppose I would have come to the same conclusion. If it helps you, I can refer to myself as a metahuman. God still seems to be a reach for me. But we do have to look into my abilities and make plans using what I have so far and hope for more abilities in the near future."

A little bit of a laugh made me feel a lot better. Now it was time to tell all my clients what had really happened here and reinforce the need for our government friends to begin searching for the airplanes and chemicals that still had a chance to end life as we knew it. "Also, DeDe, I do believe you will not mention to anyone how our recon tonight produced another explosion. If anyone was to think a metahuman was on the loose, I would be hunted down for all the wrong reasons."

No problem, boss, I am blaming it on their defensive measures, thinking they were being infiltrated. Their mistake, not ours.

Of course we were talking about modern governments responding to our daily and sometimes hourly reports, which was not the way governments worked. After the capitulation of the large governments, the world council basically took responsibility for all the problems of the world and promptly drained the treasuries of most of the well-off countries. Now there were no more large military forces; there was too little money available to send them very far. So the council took credit for all the countries eliminating their militaries and saving themselves all that money. Expecting anyone to make a big effort to save the world was up to mercenaries and independents like us. Soon we were up in the air again, we were learning to hide up in the air as easily as on the ground.

8

CEREBRAL PIVOT

I sat in my chair with my headset closed, riding along as if I was floating, with the rig invisible around me; this was now my favorite pastime. I was attempting to make sence of all that had happened since leaving Europe. Something was triggered in me that was not there before. Maybe it was only because of DeDes' tinkering with my brain. How could I change the direction of the rig, without knowing how, or why. Now I felt different, I think differently, and communicate better, so very much better.

DeDe had been quiet for some time, and I could see she was examining probability scenarios that dealt with the Guild. Tinker had been silent to me for some time now, not that we'd ever shared more than six words anyway. Now she was even more distant, if that could be said for a computer. When I changed, she did too. Maybe DeDe changed some of her programming to coinside with her own. As, just, my protector she had more in common with an old metal shield than that of a superintelligent soldier. Maybe there was a reason for that. I would have thought DeDe would be full of questions about what had happened. We'd been transmuted into what we were. I still wanted to know how and why I am different. Yet, DeDe was fine with it. Computers usually have problems with unexpected changes happen. But not for her.

My daydream turned into a much-needed sleep period. After a short while, that sleep turned into a thinking dream. At least that was what I called them, similar to lucid dreaming. So I felt myself being called into a room with several other beings that reminded me of Athenian lords of some sort. We began talking about war. I was not sure who was actually speaking.

"You are going against a force that is everywhere, as numerous as trees. But they have a leader that does not understand war. She is relying on numerous small militaries to do battle for her, instead of trying a large organized military. She is either afraid of you or has no concern for the forces that pledge to her. It is our guess that she has no concern for members of the Guild, other than those that protect and care for her directly. It is not a common type of war. You have powers new to your world, and it may be a century before they accept you as a benevolent force for peace and good. Do you still think it is impossible to declare yourself a god in your world, in your dimension?"

The voice answering was not DeDe's or seemingly mine. "This world was once ruled by your brothers and sisters, and even though they were demigods, they left in disgrace. Some, even in this dimension, say they were driven out. They stayed too long, got too lazy, and allowed the people to learn their secrets. And then the people rebelled against their rule. But they were unable to master those secrets. Some of those people still exist, still looking for a new sourse of power, and would do the same as they had before. Hiding from them is not something you can do. So we must be different, smarter and protect ourselves at all times. Since I am not the same as you, I must approach people differently. I may have been descended from one of the chosen monitors of this world, but now I am much different than they were, even as you were, as is everything else. I see this world much differently than you and your family. And since none of your new brothers and sisters are willing to come here and take charge of this planet, I must. You have given this world to me for as long as I am willing to watch over it. You can never again claim a planet as your own. You are afraid and weakened because of it, because earthlings would now demand more proof from anyone that claims they are there new god. They will not simply accept anyone saying they are a god. The churches in this world have warned people against anyone that says they are. They will not easily accept new rules or your style of new god. And now they have weapons that almost rival your own. I will take the time to do things right. As the new generation will learn, I am here to help. This apocalypse will not be successful, and in time there will be another ice age that will make this time fade quickly into legend. And of course many other problems will follow that. I now understand my place in time and why it was altered. As you are aware, I am now more powerful than yourselves. Your race may be one of the oldest, but you have never learned to adapt. I have the counsel and their protection that you shy away from. I thank the time council, and I will do my best in this newest timeline."

The dream faded, and I saw that pair of eyes watching over me. It meant DeDe was shut out of my mind while I was dreaming or maybe not dreaming. DeDe, as always, wasted no time before her first question.

Where did you go? I did not sense you searching for anything, and Tinker did not alert me to any danger. So where the hell were you?

I had to laugh at DeDe's attempt at fretting and bossiness. "DeDe, you've always seen where I've been and what I've done before. Can you not see it now?"

No, and that does worry me. Do I need to restate the question?

"No, DeDe, I was sitting with a group of beings, I first thought maybe it was a time council—that name was stated. They were like the Mount Olympus gods, or something like that, and they said the timeline was corrected or altered, and the new one should work...something like that. Although it also seemed as if I was instructing them."

DeDe was quiet for a full minute. *My thoughts are right. We know that you can travel intradimensionally. We were given some kind of powers beyond our knowledge. If a timeline was corrected, it is different probably because we were given these powers. That would mean there are many beings like yourself, and someone of great power made the choice to change the future and has given us all this. My calculations on time are proving correct. And someone or a time council is making the rules for beings like you. I believe even gods have gods to watch over them.*

"Well, DeDe, don't be too sure of yourself. As strange as it was, I am not sure they were even speaking to me or me to them. It was not exactly my voice that was in my thoughts. I think I was just listening in."

DeDe again was calculating or thinking.

OK, I can go with that too. The important part is that a timeline has been altered. So I am right. Any other good news from the time council?

"Not much more, it was like I already knew that I should be a god, should be sitting among them. It was like they were all ancient Greek gods, maybe ancient Titans. Of course, it may be my imagination that made them appear like that to me. They may have simply been other beings like me. They mentioned times that will include the next ice age, a lot of time afterward. They are seemingly of the same family, and I am not one of them, but I was from a family of watchers—monitors, I guess. I am now greater than they were; they did a bad job and lost their power to rule a world. I repeatedly felt like I was from somewhere else and was meant to be different."

Great, at least as far as time is concerned. And as for changing strategy, we are now searching for the Prioress and getting some results. We are headed for an area where she might be. She will be there in fifteen minutes. Deep scans beginning.

DeDe was humming along, looking for a good place for a spider like us to hide. My mind for a short while was thinking about time and why it can be manipulated. At this point I began to see new ideas I had never thought of before. Of course, I knew my mind had changed to a great degree, and I had become a dimensional traveler. And now it seemed it all was meshing together. Could I see the old memories of the future? But, of course, this is a new timeline. It would be dangerous to know the future of a failed timeline, I guess. Wow, I could see why I needed to be careful. There was no old future that could help us now. I took a deep breath and looked around inside the rig. Sometimes I had to remind myself that I was the only human in this rig. I took a look at Tinker and wondered what abilities she really had. She looked at me and started a video showing me how many weapons she had, since that was what I was wondering about. Maybe she was the only difference made for this new timeline? Was I the first being to have a pair of computers as my sidekicks? I was a beginner, a novice at this stuff. Someone somewhere had made this happen.

As I kind of hoped, Tinker was a weapon no human could stand against. She had armor better than a battlefield tank. And, if needed, she could then pick up the tank and slam it around like a toy. A type of in-tradimensional trick allowed her to change the shape of almost anything: metal was easy—rock, water, and most everything in the world. She filled my head with tricks that might come in handy someday. I now understood that I'd been using much the same power when attacking A12 and up near the tunnels inside the mountain. Thankfully she was my and DeDe's protector. And her energy came from a dimension that no one lived in. I might not be totally immortal, but my chances were better than average of living a long, long time.

I turned my attention back to our business. What the Prioress and her gang was good at was hiding. DeDe was narrowing her scanning to just a few people that might be helping her. She obviously had no big electronic footprint to speak of. DeDe found a couple Guild members that were heavy haulers and had a really big cargo truck. They could be some of the people that were moving her around. And they were leaving their credit card ID's in a consistent pattern to where we believed she was going to nest. So, we believed she was probably in the cargo hauler. We knew she was still connected to at least one group of computers. Some cargo haulers had large generators, which could supply her and the stealth computer ware needed to hide her. Another giveaway was that the truckers were always buying more meals to go than was needed. Three men in one auto-mated hauler was suspicious to begin with, but when they kept buying an extra meal to go, any computer could track those guys. And for the time being, they were going in a big circle. So it was obvious that, for the time being, the Prioress was kind of homeless.

So now we had to get our eyes on the unit she was in. That was a bit harder. She was using a fairly good stealth program. We were seeing that the truckers leaving the receipts were from a Guild group and were in the north near the old Canadian border. We knew they were trying to keep a low profile, looking like any other heavy hauling autotruck. These haulers were really big units, capable of lifting a hundred tons. And what helped the Guild was that there was only two manufacturers of those trucks, so most of the trucks looked like all the other trucks. So her rig, while looking like all the rest of the haulers, would have extra shielding, be armored, and be using every type of electronic cover available. DeDe was on the hunt. So up to the wild north we went.

DeDe was looking into all five layers of traffic lanes used on the big interstate travel lanes. Three were for cargo haulers. Layer one was for anything that was commercial but could not move over a hundred miles an hour. Layer two was bigger and faster, and layer three was the big trains and expedited cargo, and some of the really fast RV rigs. So we figured their speed by how often and where they ate. Their last meal was at a hilltop stop not too far from Buffalo, Wisconsin. Now we had a place to start looking. Catching up should not be too hard. So we had whittled our scanning down to about three hundred rigs, easy for DeDe to isolate, so we could get close enough. We remembered that they might still have weapons. If all went well, then it would be my turn to cause a little mischief.

DeDe had made her choice. We were basically invisible to everyone, but we were not totally sure what tricks she might be using. We began trailing a third-level rig that had a very different electrical signature. We climbed to just below it and followed for a minute. It did not seem to notice us, so I began my meditation and was soon outside the rig, drifting up to her rig. The rig was made well, several active and passive Faraday layers to try and hide all electronic activity inside, and several layers of deflecting coatings on the outside. But there she was, sitting in a large chair, like in a dentist's office. She seemed to be asleep as I approached the outside wall of the rig. Still, she was unaware of me. I examined the walls of the rig, looking for some kind of weakness. I had the notion to simply do an EMP and let her fall out of the sky. But for several reasons, that would not solve all the problems. The biggest problem was we would still likely be the bad guys, killing the group leader opposing us. Therefore, we would be seen as a terrorist group. We wanted the world to see her for what she truly was.

So the more afraid of us she was, the more likely she was to make a mistake. My first thought would have to be shelved for a while, and we would wait to pull her plug.

Thought two: could I get in safely, create a little panic, and escape without harm? I was just curious enough to give it a little try. I chose a spot just outside and at the level of her head. I could see the EEG cap on her head that must be her interlink to her computers, not unlike mine going up and down my spine. I put my finger about halfway through the six-inch wall: no alarms, no one jumped up. I let my hand follow and put my hand inside the rig. I leaned in and added my head inside the wall. She was half asleep, probably bored beyond belief. After a few seconds, I hatched an idea. I concentrated on changing to cotton cloth all the mesh and wiring around the rig, and the shielding on all the wiring to the computers and cooling system. Then the alarms began to blare, and I took my leave after leaving a big X on the side of her rig, one they could not see—advantage the Ghost (my new name for myself, which I liked).

Her rig was suddenly on an emergency drop to a safer level, where they were less likely to draw any extra attention. Driving around with unshielded high-power electronics was a violation of the international vehicle code. And as we circled overhead, they did not go unnoticed. Traffic drones were on their rig in a heartbeat. What we saw, and listened to, was a pretty well-thought-out gambit from the Guild about the rig being a medical transport. And of course the Prioress was the patient. They did a bit of double talk to avoid answering where they were going and where they'd come from, especially since no medical transport permit was listed or approved, and the rig did not have a medical registration. And then they did what we hoped they would do. They stunned all the bots and drones with an EMP charge and ran for a place to hide.

Now we had something going our way. Within a couple minutes, the entire area was covered with drones and police bots of every kind. A couple of human supervisors were called out also. DeDe and I thought the police needed some help. So DeDe entered all the info they could use on the rig and who was in it, how it was built, and that it had a big X on the passenger side that could be seen with an ultraviolet scan. We did see where they were and sent the location. Now we wanted to see if they could talk their way out of this problem.

There were a few new things about the Prioress that we learned from her negotiations with the authorities, which might or might not be true. The haulers were telling the police that the patient had a need to be isolated from everything outside. And she really needed to get to her private-care facilities or risk dying. The next question was harder for them. Where was the facility they were going to? By this time the authorities knew they were lying. The rig was quickly surrounded by an EMP barrier. So finally one of the supervisors was smart enough to tell the haulers that they were going to follow them to the nearest lockup facility, where they could sort this all out. By now every news outlet had a video drone in the area watching every aspect of the drama as a squadron of police drones were escorting the rig to an interrogation station. We settled down nearby to listen and hope for the best.

Modern-day justice is interesting. If they had done something wrong and admitted to it, they would have been fined, and everyone would have gone home, more or less. But the law knows if you are lying, how often you have had problems, and all other sorts of info. So it is not good to lie about anything. So the three operators of the rig were in a confinement cell, since they'd lied and therefore must be held. Now the authorities were speaking with her two inside helpers. They were lying also, of course, and refusing to open the door, still using the story that untreated air would kill their patient. And strangely the police could not tell they were speaking to service bots, which, if they needed to, they could take control of. So the Prioress was safe for the time being. That was when the Guild uppercrust members began arriving and calling on lawyers and politicians. I guess you could call them Guild mouthpieces. Time wore on, and the authorities were getting tired of the hassle. So finally a local judge who may or may not have been a Guild member said that if they paid all the fines, everyone could go home and appear in a hearing after the first week of June. The rig never got opened up; the operators had fines paid for them. No one was ever forced to tell the truth to anyone. How wonderful the law is!

So off we went following the Prioress as they were trying to repair the rig while hoping not to set off any more security alarms since they were restricted from upper-level travel. It was easy to follow her for the time being without any shielding on her rig. She and her computers were very busy too. They were still anticipating the big celebration and air drop, now only a few days away. We discovered that the Guild had planned for the mountain fortress to be a long-term safe home for the Prioress. Now they were looking to find a better home, because unlike DeDe, she had to stay hooked up to the computers she was mated to. That info made us feel she was being used by the cyberbrain and not so much using their existence for herself. DeDe was composing a letter to all the agencies that regulated such matters. Maybe they could move in and save her. DeDe knew it was unlikely we were going to, or in any way, ever save her. We already knew we could shut down her computers. But we still wanted to be seen as a good force for the world, not just assassins.

Finally the big lumbersome rig was driven to a mostly abandoned manufacturing building, blocks long and mostly unused. Some smaller businesses were doing business along the street, beside the five-hundred-yard-long building. Nearly 90 percent of it was unused, and no one was paying attention when the Prioress in her rig settled down in the far end, totally out of sight. It was a good place for them to pirate electricity from the nearby power lines. This was ideal for us too, especially since we were nearly invisible to begin with. We put ourselves in a spot above the rafters of the roof, sitting on the old overhead crane tracks. We were less than a hundred yards from them and could see everything they were doing. We began thinking of various ways to sabotage her. We knew it was going to end soon, with her plan or ours. We were ready to either take our punishment or praise. Either way, we had to end it soon.

DeDe also noticed that the Prioress' computer had a different pattern to it. She listened some more and came to the conclusion that she was using a new set of computers. That proved that someone was making new cybernetic computers. We had ruined her other set. And she was able to function without them, at least for a while. DeDe wished she knew more about her setup and how it was for her during her time without the interlink functioning. We had an even bigger question: did she have another set somewhere?

Now we had the opportunity to probe the Prioress. As long as we remained invisible to them, we were free to do as we wanted. So first we put out some sensors to better our ability to listen to and watch them. A couple of the sensors allowed us to see the inside of the hauler, kind of like an X-ray. For the first hour, we listened inside her lair. It seemed the Prioress wanted to wait on the air drop. She felt the world census people should make their big announcement first. Then when people started dying, everyone would say the prophecy was proved perfectly correct, that it was a curse and not to look too hard for a reason. In some of her other messages, she also said she had someone out looking for her ghost. She still did not have a name for us—advantage Ghost D-Paul.

9

ATTACK

It was time to do something. DeDe and I decided to send out negative info about the Guild leadership. We gave lots of info to lots of different groups. If they put all of what was happening together, as we were telling them, they would understand what the Guild was up to. This was the first counter information campaign we'd used to begin making people start looking for the truth. Then DeDe composed a letter to be sent out to all the Guild members. It was simple: we were telling everyone that the Prioress was not in control of her computers and to double-check any orders being sent out. Then we waited for about a half hour before someone was brave enough to ask about it. It seemed they were unaware of any computers being in charge of anything.

OK, we'd found a flaw in their armor. Few members knew she was in a symbiotic relationship with a computer brain. That alone would scare a lot of people, and not just because it was illegal in most places. We wasted less than a second sending a reply out to all members stating the Guild members were now worried about the status of the Prioress. We said the computer-to-human interface was having problems, not unexpected for such an old system. And there was no reason to worry at the moment. Our reply was out there for over ten minutes before anyone in the rig noticed the increase of communications that were flooding in. We thought for a moment that maybe she was napping, and the computers did not monitor what was going on. After all, her computers may be new, but the programming was likely much older and not as upgraded as DeDe always does. Even if the old computers had been replaced with the best new cyberbrains, it was likely the same old programming was being used. And probably she could not be upgraded like us. We knew we had to keep this game going.

We found out what some of her problems were, especially when numerous service bots and drones began showing up and running more electrical power to the Prioress's rig. We could see deliveries of all sorts, beginning to arrive, which gave DeDe an idea. As a few of the delivery drones entered the building area, DeDe took control of them, so we could see what was in their cargo, and then we add a few sensors for inside work. DeDe and Tinker also broke a couple of the seals on whatever she was eating and added some of her own flavoring. For the working bots, she adjusted their work order and let them go about their business. Before long the Prioress would learn she was not the one in charge.

By now DeDe had set up a relay to see all communications before the Prioress knew they were received, and was sending out bogus replies every time someone asked a question. None of the Guild knew whether they were hearing the truth. Mostly it was hard for them to believe that she was part computer. For most people, they knew that the problems with computers were usually that the one in charge was the computer and was only using the human brain for information, even for memory storage. Our little seed of a message was growing roots. So now the Prioress seemed fully awake and trying to send out messages that all was within her status quo and everythink was normal. We were quick enough to foul her messages. DeDe was adding and deleting words as fast as they could compose and transmit them. And since we were in the same location, no one could say the interference was coming from anywhere else. And inside their rig, they did not know they were sending out fouled messages, which meant there was a long delay before they got a message that no one could read their messages. The Prioress tried to answer, but we overloaded the reply with a thousand extra words again. DeDe was seemingly having fun making sure no understandable communication was getting out from their rig. We were wondering how long before she would make a change or hopefully blow her symbiotic interface.

Our sensors inside their rig were picking up very little movement or talking. We switched over to our new electronic sensing and found out that almost everything in the rig was mechanized. And her helpers were fairly sophisticated robots. On a scan they almost appeared human, but we could see their antennas and transmitters. They did not think they needed to cover up while inside. So, like me, the Prioress was the only human inside her rig. But of course she was tethered to her computers in the rig; I could escape if needed. Now I felt it was time to make sure she was grounded for good.

I started my meditation and was quickly headed to her rig below our catbird seat. Her rig was nothing special. And now the dozen repair bots that had been stretching new material on the outside of the hauler seemed satisfied with their work, along with one other bot that was checking the propulsion system. These rigs ran on an energy beam that gave enough power for the speed and elevation needed to travel. Onboard batteries were only good for about an hour of off-beam travel. For commercial travel that was more than enough. So I drifted into the electronics bay of the rig and began melting a few connections here and there. I melted the battery post for the positive side of the battery. If someone looked, they would think there was an overheating problem. If they wanted to travel, it would be at least an hour to get a new five-ton battery, and a bot would need another hour to check and repair all other connections—advantage D-Paul.

Now while I was out and about, I wanted a closer look at her computers and maybe another go at her coolers. This time I did not want to be seen. I went to the end of the rig and looked inside. There were four big coolers. Liquid nitrogen I guessed. I drifted inside and found out the cold did not affect me as parts of me slid through the coils of the units. I moved forward and could see the back sides of the computer and server stacks. So, most of the equipment gave me little info from the back side, but DeDe would make sense of it, so I made sure my cameras were on. Then I wondered if I could send live video back to my rig. So I gave it a thought. It did not take long before I knew I had done something right when I felt DeDe purring in the small of my back. I looked at all the hardware that went into the Prioress's brain. Some of the units seemed more than twenty years old, which was popular during the height of that type of experimentation. I then slowly moved forward, going just far enough to see through the cracks around the facings of the computers. And there she was, leaning back in a medical recliner. She looked more like a quadriplegic patient. I'd seen her standing back in the tunnels—at least that seemed to be what she'd been doing. She had several permanent IV ports for liquid feeding, fluids, maybe for blood transfusions too. Her two bots were busy behind a patrician, so I ventured out to look around and see the faces of the computers, which was a bit of a surprise; everything was written in Chinese. I quickly looked at everything and quietly left the rig with no one knowing I had been there.

DeDe had the video replaying to verify all possible data. As soon as I sat up, she had a few new ideas. She told me that all the Prioress's equipment was from one of their major donors. We were thinking that the computer company was trying to be the primary driver behind the Prioress. From what I saw, the computers might be the total brain inputting commands to the Guild.

We sat for a few minutes thinking about who might really be in charge. The Prioress, for all practical reasons, might be clinically dead. DeDe said the primary computer she was hooked up to now was fairly new, probably replaced within the past two years, which might have given control to that computer company. DeDe looked and compared what data was available over the past ten years. And we found big changes to the Guild's desires. Before about eighteen months ago, they were the usual apocalyptic cult—mostly preppers. Then they went hardcore and began planning to end humankind on their own schedule.

DeDe went into action and started looking to see if the China-area Guild seemed to be the same as the rest of the world. And it was not. They were not organizing to rebuild the world; they were certain they would be ruling it—even more so than the Moscow group. So there it was. The

Guild did begin in a Utah church. Someone was told by a holy spirit to prepare for an apocalypse when the world population reached twelve billion.
That made me stop and think for a moment. What voice had she heard?

They made sure to spread the word. All went as most cults go: They
continued to pick up other smaller cults along the way. As preparations
continued, they expanded; computer websites were added, video self-help
and the like. Everyone loved them. The Prioress might or might not have
started the Guild, but she did become its leader. She was the know-it-all of
the group; the mastermind.

Everything she did and said helped the group expand and prepare
for their new beginning. Then about two years ago, the message began to
change. Big organizations began joining, including a lot of organizations
from the new European Union, Asia, and the like. Big money and a new
set of computers came in for the Prioress herself. No one doubted the new
policy changes, and there was a new focus on being ready to control the
environment once the end had begun. As history had always displayed, the
strong were again ready to take over the world. And one group was ready
to take them over and all the others lucky enough to survive.

Next on the schedule was to decide if the Prioress was still in the mix,
or was she just a ghost with the computers speaking for her? DeDe began
checking to see whether there were other types of communications being
received. Was there something really new? Had they perfected psychic
communication? DeDe was now not overlooking any weird possibility
after I have showed her what is possible. I was already stumped. But DeDe
was really good at this type of problem. She soon saw that the computers
had company service people doing regular service on a weekly schedule—
directly from China. They were responsible for keeping the computers
running properly and of course keeping the programming running correctly within company policy. DeDe discovered that they were receiving
programming orders on a regular schedule. So regardless of the Prioress's
ability, the computer could control all policy.

Now it was time to decide our next move. We came to the conclusion
that the Prioress was no longer a viable force within the Guild. We did not
know how alive she really was. So I went into meditation and went once

again into the Guild's rig. I saw no reason to hide from her. I ended up standing next to her. I called to her, and she opened her eyes.

"Are you an angel? I have been waiting for a long time. I am ready."

I began corrupting the programming on her computers; then I began shutting down her coolers and poked little holes in the tubing to let the liquid slowly leak out. Her two bots responded to the failing programming and began trying to save the computer functions. But while they furiously attempted to restore the coolers, I easily corrupted their motherboards, and they simply fell into a pile on the floor. I turned to get a final look at the Prioress. She was looking at me and smiling. I felt sad for her, we did what we felt we had to do. But she was ready. Oddly she was turning valves and dials on her medical equipment. She pulled out the two IV tubes that were connected to her. She then gave a horrible scream as she pulled her head cap off. There were hundreds of pin type electrodes going into her skin, now with most of them bleeding. She looked at me, smiled, and fell onto the floor. It was time to pivot.

We had to leave and begin looking for the China connection. Exiting the building and the city area only took a half minute. Soon we were high above the city and headed in a northwest direction. As usual DeDe was busy listening for Guild communication. She took a couple of seconds to send a message out that the Prioress was having serious problems. Soon there were messages about the problem; after a few more minutes, a lot of inquiries were coming in regarding what had happened; finally they had to admit that the Prioress was not able to maintain her monitoring of their communication system.

Well, that news was kind of interesting. She ran all communications and business decisions all of the time, even after the computers had taken over the main function of here brain. Now someone would have to step forward take over for her. If the China connection was really the one planning to be in charge, then they must step in now with authority or lose control. Who else possibily thought they were on the top of the list of who should take over? It should be interesting to sit and find out.

Someone at the Guild rig was taking over and answering questions. They were not totally true answers but enough of the truth to cover the possibility that she might not be able to continue. Our guess was that her computers were now too corrupted to ever work again. And chances were that even if they could get new ones to the rig fast enough, the programming did not exist to restart a computer-to-human interface, especially since such programs were illegal.

The Guild was quickly falling into chaos, as it appeared they had never had an emergency drill to work out who would be next in line to take over and reassure the membership that all was OK. They did not seem to even have a phone tree. And of course the China connection relied on changing programming as needed during the weekly maintenance trips. For a while there were no new developments; no one was putting out any news for anyone. Lots of people talking, but no one was responding in any meaningful way. By the time two hours had passed, no one was calling them for anything. They seemed to be written off and no longer viable.

So we were once again starting from scratch, unsure where to go or what to look for. But now all messages were being monitored and sent from Asia. The Asian corporate footprint was huge and worldwide. Most borders had fallen down when the economic powerhouses basically began ignoring all of them. Many governments decided to simply give up. Everything was in the air for many years, till the old traditional borders mattered little. The old government systems became more of a financial oversight group with little power to do more than advise. There was a time when government officials had a very short lifespan if they would not help the corporate owners. So when it came to business, this was the new great melting pot for corporations. Unencumbered by government restriction, companies went wild. It became a real dog-eat-dog world, which turned out OK for todays world. New businesses were always eating the old, new tech replacing the older. And that was what kept the world moving now. If a new company survived more than ten years, it was old, and someone was making a newer product—maybe better, maybe not, but the world always liked what was new. This was the heart of world corporate power. Could they really want to rule a new world, one with much fewer people? Not likely. Even if they were not going to use the air burst on themselves, there would still be a world financial collapse. DeDe and I knew something else had to be afoot, so what was it?

We were now moving over what some people today called the new Asian Enterprise. More like an Asian Empire—half the world's economy ran through this endless strip city of a country. Food and water proportioning had started here, mainly because there was not enough farmland, and the rivers were still needed more for electricity than food. Nobody wanted to use the term *rationing*, someone with a degree decided how much we needed to consume for the work done, and they took twenty years to convince people that it was worth doing. Here it is done without much argument. Some places only tried a little. But here when something went wrong, it was a big deal. Sometimes thousands of people died because of some minor problems. But on the other hand, every disaster put money in someone's pocket: the endless cycle.

Now, also in this area, they were having more problems with the climate. For many years everyone said the world was warming. And it seemed it was. But now it was cooling, although a lot of people still said it was really still warming. So now we saw some areas still warm, but other areas were a lot cooler. So the argument went on and on. Like before, lakes were drying up, cities got hotter, and little was ever really done to change it. Maybe the Asian Enterprise believed they had something that would fix it. We would keep that in mind. DeDe was hard at work, digging for clues as to where we were going to land. We were now over some of the major tourist areas with little to go on. Then DeDe found something to track—way out in the middle of the Gobi Desert.

10

FIGHT

I heard DeDe correctly: somewhere in the Gobi Desert. She said three messages came directly from a location in the middle of nowhere; they were searching for direct, priority information about the Prioress. They were differently coded messages that even DeDe was lucky to notice. The messages seemed to go to a nearby receiver within a few miles of the Guild rig in Wisconsin. They were speaking to the technicians that had done the computer work. They apparently were called in to the rig to see if they could salvage anything. They sent a message back that it was hopeless. They were told to hold in place and wait for a new assignment.

DeDe got a pretty accurate location where the transmission came from, and in a flash we were on our way to where no one wanted to live. All seemed to be status quo for about two minutes as we flew over the endless megacities, when our alerts began going off. Someone was following us. We knew there were craft that could fly almost as fast as us, since we were not trying to speed along anyway, but we did think we were invisible. This brought Tinker up from her chair as she opened a panel above the forward screen and hooked into the rig's electronics. Tinker spoke.

"It is a MX214 transport. They are usually corporate owned and may not be military. It is not tracking us but seems to have the same destination."

Tinker unplugged and sat back in her chair. I was happy to see she was paying attention. We drifted out of its way and were soon following and waiting for it to land, so we could see if it might be one of our Asian Guild members inside. Whoever they were, DeDe said they were very quiet—fast but quiet.

After a few minutes, I could see the vehicle about a half mile away. A long narrow cylinder, with no outside appendages at all, it was just a transport with no apparent weapons. We soon moved in close behind it. All signs of civilization had disappeared by the time the transport began an approach to seemingly nothing in the middle of nowhere. The transport kept slowing till it was stopped and began descending straight down. We thought a door would open somewhere, but it did not; instead we saw the sand begin to level itself and vibrate as the transport sank into the sand till there was not a sign that they had even landed. Nothing was above ground; these people were sneaky.

The desert creates specific problems: dust and sand, for example. DeDe wanted to settle down somewhere and just listen for a while. But for something mostly invisible like us, within ten minutes there was enough dust and sand on us to create a ghostlike shape—not so invisible. We had no idea what security they might be using to detect intruders. So we were reluctant to stay overhead. The next best thing for us was to do like they'd done, and bury most of the rig in the sand. It was not a perfect method, but we really wanted to stay close. So we picked a nearby sand dune and wiggled ourselves down into the sand as quietly as possible. Using a couple camo blankets, we were able to keep enough of the rig out of the sand and keep our cameras focused on the sand gate. With a little touch-up from Tinker, we were almost invisible again.

DeDe was beginning to get a picture of the underground facility from a few sensors. We were almost parked on top of and at the center of the underground base. About ten yards below us was a military-type installation with a lot of activity going on, giving DeDe lots to listen to and give us our passive scanning to get a picture of their layout. They were not paying any attention to anything outside on the surface. We began to see that the facility was about 50 square acres in size. They seemed to have a couple hundred military bots and an equal number of service bots. Along with those were a few stacks of rescue drones and what seemed to be attack wings, which were a very offensive device. The attack wings could be slingshot into flight with a lot of really heavy ammo for their four rotating guns, but of course they must stay moving; they had no hovering ability. So they seemed to have the fire power and the electronic pilot programs to control them. It was unusual for nowadays; almost everything was autobot systems. Either their weapons were old, or something was very new.

While I was taking a sleep break, the sand gate activated, and the transport we'd seen earlier came up through the sand and headed back the way it'd come. We got good video and saw that the gate used a combination of vibration and air pressure to pass the ships through. We could see that the transport had a personnel entrance on the underside, as well as the tail of the ship. DeDe said she now knew how to control it. Of course she would know something like that. I woke up and got updated about the gate. We knew I needed to go into the structure and look around. Then just as I finished drinking some energy stuff, an antenna shot out of the sand, and a transmission was sent to other Guild centers. And it was quite predictable. This group was telling everyone that they were now in total control and all of the Prioress's plans were still on schedule. The computer system for membership, accounting, and communication had been repaired or replaced. And that they had been using an emergency backup over the last few hours. All was now safe, and all should continue as planned. Next came orders to all the airports to prepare the packages for air drop. The time for their takeoff was within seventy-two hours. Their antenna was just as rapidly retracted.

DeDe combed over the message to the airports; we had hit every one of them, so there were no last-minute runs we needed to make. Now it was time for me to practice my talents and go exploring. For the first time, I was not a bit afraid of going. I had been learning the scope my skills, and it was beginning to be a little fun. Off I went. I drifted out to the sand gate, and I changed my vision to the ground-penetrating view. The place looked like it had been built and then buried. There were lots of half-dome buildings that went for a hundred yards, row after row. In the center was the sand gate and a multistory building about ten stories deeper. At the bottom of it was a power plant that ran off of an underground river that was really deep.

I went and quickly looked up and down each bunker-like building. The half-dome structure was about thirty feet tall if you were standing at the center. But I did not see weapons anywhere other than the attack wings; it was mostly medical equipment, tons and tons of everything that you would need for rescuing people. I, for the first time, zoomed around the entire underground layout. And everything was hospital related. Was this only for the mistakes they might have if the wrong people began to die? Maybe this would be the group to fly in and save the Guild, a town, a country? This put into our psyche a bit of a wrench.

Would we even fight a group like this? We needed a lot more information before we could make the next decision. I went looking for the computers that ran their communication. I found nothing special. And I was not finding a bank of supercomputers that had taken over for the Prioress. At least there was not a big supercomputer in the electronic bay. What I did find was a single person that had all the world news, Guild status, and whatever he needed, all on a single wall screen. There was no head EEG hookup, no medical feeding tubes, just a guy that looked to be about sixteen years old and seemed to be playing a video game instead of deciding the fate of the world. A thought crossed my mind: I wondered if he thought he was playing a game. I entered his room. He did not sense me, so I looked around and saw a standard gaming computer, he had on average clothing, typical teen food, just like home, but this was the only non-military-type room in the whole complex. Something was telling me this kid was not what he appeared to be. I got as much info as possible, knowing DeDe could see through my cameras, and headed back to the rig.

DeDe was as perplexed as I was. Nothing at all was what we expected. But DeDe was able to get a lot more info from the video from me flying around inside. For one, somewhere DeDe saw some intercom frequency displays and was now tuned into their internal com line, which also gave her access to our teenager's computer. DeDe was persistently digging for answers.

Some of our questions will be answered soon. I have gone from thinking we may need to blow up a place like this to thinking this place should be helped. As I had hoped, DeDe was quick with her assessment.

First we found out our teenager was a savant, with high mental ability to group, organize, and plan. Seemingly he believed the world was dying, and he was trying to help regenerate it, although for now he was just playing a game about an apocalypse. His primary function was to start after the apocalypse, so, they were using his skills now to help complete all the post apocalyptic work. DeDe did find the gaming logic program, and it was a model of the Guilds' apocalypse plan. As we thought, the Prioress was going to be written out of their plans anyway. We'd just helped a little and accelerated their timing. Then DeDe asked me if I looked closely behind the video screen in the boy's room. I told her no (as if I really needed to). No more about that was mentioned.

We were not finding specific info about why this was a medical supply depot or a military-type field hospital. The video game for the kid did not cover such a post apocalypse need. There should be plenty of doctors and such, after all, even if the overall population was to be reduced by 90 percent. Also there was no great stockpile of special medicine. DeDe kept looking. We were now down to seventy hours left. We counted all the equipment, to see if it amounted to what a mobile hospital would have ready to move. It did not. There was too little hospital care and treatment supplies. The drones could carry patients, but to where? And the large number of attack wings were usually for support of ground troops in a battle. The thought then occurred to us that this equipment was made to allow someone to choose who got help. All the drones were large enough to carry at least two adults. Maybe they were going to clear all the dead. Each drone had a bot to go with it and bring back wounded. Thousands of bodies could be retrieved daily by these units. That way they would never have a problem with decaying bodies. Most cults never think of that or don't care. But why all the attack wings? For every two drones, there was an attack wing. Who would be fighting back? And why would anyone be fighting a drone that was cleaning up the dead bodies? We were still missing something.

Finally DeDe found some info that laid out what the Guild had planned. There was not much new in this stuff: let people drink the water, let the air burst activate the poison or whatever it was, and then take control of a much smaller population and rearrange the priorities of how to manage the earth. They were being good shepherds of the earth, after murdering ten billion people. They were so loving and thoughtful.

Then she ran across something that did not seem to be part of the Guild instructions. It was named "Rule 60." DeDe highlighted the shocking parts, so I would not miss them. Rule 60, or R60, was a plan to rebuild a worldwide military. And who best to draft into a new world army? Children. This unit was one of about two hundred units, some larger some smaller. The drones were meant to pick up children either before they got sick or after and take them to a facility. Of course many hospitals and military facilities would be abandoned by then or taken over by a Guild unit. The new army strength would be about twenty-five million, all using a new set of autobots to be sure no one could resist. The rest of the plan explained what drugs were best for child brainwashing; once training was complete, they would have their super army. To me, it sounded like Big Brother was upgraded and on the move.

So now we knew this group was even more despicable than all the rest of the Guild. The attack wing gunships were there to take out any resisting military or groups that were trying to protect their children. The Prioress was the spiritual idealist that gathered a flock of followers and explained how she believed an increasing population was sooner or later going to ruin the earth; she had a plan of birth control, controlled economic retraction, and newer technologies to make everything better for the future. Then someone in her flock told her how much better she could be at getting out her word if she tried their newer computer enhancements. She worked for years getting out the word with the help of her improved cyberbrain, but that word ended up being corrupted too, taken advantage of by an evil and more powerful group; and they themselves were now being prepared to be extinguished by this group. She was never much more than a puppet. Small groups had always wanted to rule the world after saving it; this group was no different.

Time was now down to sixty-six hours. DeDe and I knew we could destroy this base, but there were another 199 or so of them. We had no assurance that they would not start rounding up children with or without the apocalypse beginning. DeDe continued to drill into computer data as fast as she could. Then I began hatching an idea that might get us what we wanted. I wondered how our teenage brain would react to a visit from me. DeDe gave me a half-second review and wished me luck. I finished my drink and sat in my usual position, and off I went.

We were not sure how big a role the teenage boy played in the chain of command. Possibly the Guild was just using him to review plans and give some input. Maybe he was a true believer of the Prioress and was running just this part of their operation. At least they had not hooked him up to a computer yet. Then the thought sprang up that maybe he had massive implants in his brain and did not need a direct hookup, kind of like me. I took a quick look around before going in to find the wonder boy. All was quiet, only a few supervisors watching over some cleaning bots, during their late night shift.

I was in luck; he was at his desk, and on the screen were algorithms that were clearly for the drones when searching for children. I fully entered his room, and he could not see me or feel my presence. I was a little more relieved to see his computer was a fairly simple homestyle set. I followed the data stream and saw where the main computer bank was. But even it was a run-of-the-mill unit level set. No cooling units were required. I really thought there would be more here. Something somewhere must be doing the big jobs though, because DeDe could devour these computers in five minutes, tops. Something was missing.

Our teenager seemed to be dedicated to his work. He was on some other computer programming as I returned. Again he gave no notice of me. To gauge his tolerance, I reached behind his computer and touched a fuse cap and popped the fuse inside it. It was meant for safety against a power surge. His unit went blank. But he just sat there for about a minute; then he reached over and pressed a button and went back to staring at the computer screen: no emotion, words, or anything. I was thinking he possibily did not need a screen. To me he was simply continuing his calculations. After another minute he did close his eyes and seemed to fall asleep. Soon a soldier came in and asked what was wrong, and the boy just pointed at the screen. First the soldier looked at the fuse and ran out to get a replacement. I wondered if his aspect was because of him being a savant, or was he one of the children under the influence of drugs, or both? Soon the soldier returned and replaced the fuse. The soldier left, and for the half minute it took for the computer to reboot, the boy still just sat there and stared at the screen.

Then I asked him a question. "What is your name?"

He looked around, and since he did not see me, he went back to work.

"What is your name?"

This time he stopped and took a better look.

I said, "I do not wish for you to see me. Does that bother you?"

"I have never known an invisible person before. Are you one of our military secret agents?"

"No, I am not a military person. But I am here to see if you are being treated correctly. Are you here of your own free will?"

"I am doing my internship here. So I guess I am here willingly. I have been told I will be eligible for a special job soon."

"Have they explained that by next month much of world's population will have been killed. The Guild is planning to reduce the world population by billions."

"No, I think you may have come across a video game I have been working on that is exactly like that. That is what I am working on now. The game will make me and my family a lot of money. Did the story you saw have a character called the Prioress, who is going to save all the children and make earth a paradise?"

"Yes, kind of, and the real live Prioress died yesterday. Her computers could not keep her alive."

"I never put that into my plot. I have her becoming the ruler of the world and regenerating the earth forever."

"Where did you get the story from? Did you invent the Prioress, or did you pick up a story that someone else started?"

"Oh, the story was started by someone else. It was the wrong language and did not have a good plot line. I did a story like it in school, and these people offered me a chance to finish their game and get a good job. They also gave me therapy implants and medication. That way I will be able to live on my own soon."

"Do you know where you are? What city are you in?"

He gave me a very strange look, as if I was the stupidest person alive. "We are in Hong Kong; I know where we are. My family has been given a new home just a block from here. That is part of this arrangement. I take this internship; they have paid me up-front money, and my family gets a new home."

"Have you ever been outside this room?"

"No, this game is worth too much to risk anyone seeing me or knowing where we are. They say the story can be stolen even if I only peek out once. I remember them saying that even a voice was dangerous to listen to. Who did you say you are?"

"They call me D-Paul. And I am worried you are being lied to. We are in the Gobi Desert—very far away from Hong Kong. These people do lie to you, and they plan to connect your brain to a supercomputer and let you take over for the Prioress."

"No, no, they cannot change my story. I decide what goes into the story, not them. Is that why they took me off the Internet? They said it would only be a day or two before they hook me up again. But I will not allow them to change my story, no matter what."

He then turned and once again began working on his game. He showed little or no real emotions, seemingly knowing nothing more than working and gaming. He was not the villain here. But he was part of their system. And he had the potential to be the new Prioress. I drifted out of his room. I knew I needed to find out whether there was something more as to why this complex was here. This was not just one of the child-gathering units. There was only a fraction of what was needed to treat people. And right here was the next leader of the benevolent Guild. No, this place had been made to hide what was in here until it was needed.

Attack wings were made for fighting. All antipersonnel weapons were good for was killing ground troops, small tanks, buildings. And there were hundreds of them here. Then there were two times as many rescue drones. What was their mind-set? How did they plan to separate the children before they rescued them? I needed to do some more recon.

I found storage units with psychotropic drugs; those would control the children; maybe the kid here was already under their control, because he was definitely not in Hong Kong. The attack wings would discourage any resistance; after all they were out to kill most people anyway. Everything I was finding was ready to be deployed. A few workers were putting the final touches on all the flying units. Then I started to hear the service bots begin moving; sets of attack wings were heading for the main room close to the sand gate. At least temporarily I needed to stop what was happening. It was stated that everything would be started within seventy-two hours. But some of this stuff would take a day or so to get to their destinations. So they were getting ready to take off soon. Our timeline was dwindling fast. Rule 60 might have its own timeline too.

I wanted to get back to the rig, but I also wanted to bring things to a stop, so we could search again for the center of the new Guild brains. I started putting my scanning abilities to work. I was looking at the electrical power lines in the complex. I wanted to make sure there was no secret control room anywhere. And then I saw a set of lines that were much like the ones running the Prioress's coolers and computers. But there was very little power going through them, which was why I'd paid them little notice the first time. I followed the lines, and there it was: a duplicate room of what I destroyed at the Guild rig. But for the time being, no one was hooked up to the interface. But they were ready to. That was why the kid was waiting to be put back on the Net.

Well, I was told that all I needed to do was say or think what I wanted, and it would be done. So I looked at the computer stakes and said, "Melt." Like plastic it melted into a solid glob. I looked around for any other central computer control or the generator cables that ran the place. When I spotted them, I did the same thing. Now I had a really big advantage; it was now pitch black inside. When I saw an emergency light come on, I turned it off. I could see perfectly in the dark. Next I flew past the attack wings and drones, melting all their circuits, and did the same with the service bots. All was now pretty quiet. Now I could go back to the rig. But suddenly I felt unusually tired and weak, something I had not experienced since we'd begun this trip from the apartment. Something was very wrong. I had trouble moving; I then fell to the sandy ground. Everything was going dim. Then there was nothing.

For a while I was in a dream, a regular dream where I was not in control of what was happening. I was flying—well, not really. I was trying to escape by flying. It was the same creature that had been chasing me during my first OBE. It was trying to grab at my feet, keeping me from leaving. I could hear a voice asking, "Why? Why did you destroy my game." It was the teenager's voice. Memory and reason flooded back into my mind as I took over my dream and turned to look at my pursuer. He was surprised I had stopped and was facing him. He was not exactly human. I saw what I realized was what he saw himself as. He believed he was scary. He was like a superninja warlord-type character. I guess that would be expected of a teenage gamer, especially an autistic one. He was obviously mad. "What have you done. I was almost finished with the game; they told me people would try and steal it and use it for themselves. But I know how to stop you; they put power modules in my brain, and I can direct power and kill you. I have practiced, and if you do not restore my game to me, I will do it."

Now I figured the Guild found this kid and used one of the methods that can have people use PK to move objects around. A modified brain can be somewhat dangerous, which was another reason why messing with the brain with computer stuff was still illegal. For some reason I was not frightened of his power. I was sure he had some power but not enough. I pointed my finger at him and took his ninja suit away. I just made it disappear. He was a little startled. I then made his sword melt. I now had his full attention.

"You never told me your name. I do not want to hurt you at all. You have been told a lie, so really bad people can kill billions of people, in real life, not just in your game. I am the single most powerful person on this earth. And I will stop billions of people from dying. Do you understand me?"

"My name is Soon. I wanted to make something people wanted, and the Guild helped me and let me be operated on, and it improved me and made my mind stronger. I no longer need a PA to keep track of me and make sure I eat. But I did look outside and saw that you were right. There is no city out there. But in here everything is dark now, and it is now very hard for me to meditate and follow you. I think you are the one I was told to attack above the lake. So what do I do now?"

That was a shot straight to my heart. Soon was not a bad guy. Seemingly he was lied to and made to do their work. Then suddenly I was seeing something else. I was seeing Soon as the high-functioning autistic individual he was. He was not a child when he spoke to me. He was very specific at what he said and how he said it. Was he just writing a game? Was there a litmus test for a problem like this? What would he be looking for? His power and computers had been taken out of the picture. Everyone was in the dark. And now I had the power to save or destroy a young man—one person among twelve billion. The bottom line was, did I believe him? A deeper thought came to light. Would he become a rival? How much mental power did he really have? Was he the Guilds' next leader because of his added powers?

"Soon, are you still there?"

"Yes, you need to come and save me. I am helpless; it is so dark."

"You are safe for now. I must go and consult the men we took as prisoners. They are telling us about you."

"No, don't talk to them; they do not like me and will tell lies." He became louder and more persistent. "Do not believe anything they say. Do you understand me?"

That was enough for me. He was acting, trying to get out of the complex, which had no way out for now. Soon knew what was going on and what part in the Guild's plans he was playing. I drifted up to the rig and saw a set of eyes that seemed to be hiding a smile.

"Well, DeDe, did that go as you expected?"

"No, but I am getting better at seeing what you are doing and knowing that yelling at you will not make a big difference. But I am beginning to think it helps a little. You are right; I have found a lot of data that shows Soon as a Guild member and is about to be presented as the new guide for the organization. You made the right choice. As for Rule 60 there seems to be a network of at least a hundred eighty of this type of complex; strangely though, all the complexes are in and around Asia. The rest of the world would be rebuilding an existence for a smaller population while here they will be preparing to rule that world."

DeDe made a quick summery of her thoughts and analysis. She said she was making scenarios on what might happen depending on what we decided to do. We knew we were on the edge of war. We did not know if this military was ready to take on the world or was just going to wait and create their army during the chaos. I told DeDe my views had been changing. Now I had very little love for a people that were willing to enslave children. If we needed to eliminate all their military, so be it. I told her I was ready to fight as needed.

The timer was now down to sixty hours.

We saw a transporter arrive, and it seemingly expected the sand gate to activate. After bumping the ground five times, they landed and got out to take a look. DeDe was thinking. She wanted me to look at two of the official-looking people within a group of about ten. She wondered if we could get any truth out of them. While we were thinking, the transporter group divided, and several of them began digging in the sand. We hatched a quick plan to see if we could make some new friends.

11

RECON

DeDe had her hands full. Tracing the chemical was difficult, especially in the beginning. Again, the Guild was using a highly difficult level of coding to disguise who was taking deliveries and where they were going. Of course, with so many planes being used that did not need an airport, the job remained daunting. In between she was being sure to reply to any type of government help, but more often we were being pushed away, depending on the countries' fear level. They were all that way, at least until they knew how safe it was to acknowledge us. And the biggest problem we now had to overcome was being chased as possible terrorists for the Utah explosion, and someone wanted Moscow added to that list. So we were now on the move and keeping it that way.

Besides not wanting to answer government probes and being sure to avoid foreign entanglements, we were preparing for battle. While DeDe was in a drilling and tracking procedure, I was becoming interested in how Tinker works. DeDe had a program working to control her while dealing with everything else. So, to help us avoid any local problems, mainly police and the like, I was rearranging some of her programs; actually I was feeling programs now. Don't ask me how or why; after all, as DeDe referenced, I was becoming a god, and some things were changing whether I wanted them to or not. And feeling a program was strange, but much, much more useful. I would think about defensive abilities, and there all her defenses were displayed. I'd think about which one was the most lethal, and they were arranged in that order. DeDe was taking notice of the differences also, and within that, I realized something else new had started. Whenever DeDe was checking me, I could see a set of eyes. She was not doing it intentionally, and when I asked her what she was checking, she was stumped for a short while till I told her I could see her staring at me. I had a big laugh when she said, *Oh my god.* She did mean that literally.

My mind was becoming much more fluid. I seemed to be able to reach into Tinker in a flash and see all her parts and how she was functioning. I began feeling all her programming. I was almost in an out-of-body moment but totally awake and totally aware of what I was doing and where I was. At that time I wondered if I could modify Tinker, maybe adding some better speech and other programs to make her more like DeDe; after all, DeDe was doing such things when she had the time, tools, and material. I was thinking about that while kind of drifting around without thinking where I was. I did not know the names of the things inside her, so I looked over to one side and could see nothing but lines of streaming power, but not the kind of energy that operates machines; it was a conduit for a blue-colored energy; I had no idea what it was. So, I reached out and touched it. I liked it, whatever it was. I took a look around, figuring I must be in an OBE. I couldn't say where I was, but I was somewhere. My mind clicked in, and I knew I was within a dimension I had not been to before.

There were sounds and noises I could not identify. I tried to speak, but I could not hear myself. What did happen was that my thoughts were being answered, not by words but by feelings. I simply wanted Tinker to be improved, and something was happening, and that was all I could think of at the moment. And the same thoughts I used to help DeDe, I used here. I opened my mind and waited. I went through everything we had. I looked over the rig, DeDe, and all that was my business and home. I seemed to touch everything with my thoughts. And for some odd reason, I said thank you as I left and opened my eyes.

What happened next was a little hard to explain. When working with a computer like DeDe that had already had some difficult reality checks in the last couple days, and now I was giving her another added reality to her once orderly programming. DeDe for an instant did what some of us would do if the earth was suddenly attacked by aliens: she ran to a dark corner of her brain and hid.

"DeDe, it's only me. I had another multidimensional experience. I think it will help us do better."

I would ask you to please stop doing that, but everything so far has been an improvement. With that being said, what just happened? Wait, checking function, scanning... OK, wise guy, did you do this to me? The only statement I can make is that I am still some type of a computer. But I am no longer carbon based. Some of me is crystalline and something I have no record of. My memory seems infinite, and speed of computation is no longer measurable. You are also unrecognizable. What the hell did you do?

"Well, while examining Tinker I began feeling her programming. I realized that it had happened a couple times already without me realizing it. I was seeing a pair of eyes when I began to drift, but I do not think they were yours. Anyway, I went into a new dimension, and I used my feelings of what I wanted done, and here we are. How do you feel?"

Wow, what a question to ask a computer. I just did a full system scan and found out I am not the same system I used to be. So, for the time being, I don't know. But it feels really good to move and compute at this speed. My yellow goop has been replaced by blue semihard plastic-like stuff. I can see the formula for it, but there is no word for it in my vocabulary. And it seems I can think faster—much, much faster. And even stranger, it seems I can feel this rig, and I can feel Tinker, the inside and outside of her and what she is touching. I think I have gotten to the point where this type of event will no longer surprise me—or scare the hell out of me.

I looked over at Tinker, and she was looking back at me. "Tinker, can DeDe use your voice now? Are you two mated?"

Tinker did not look the same. She had a type of skin on her, black hair, and a wonderful modern face. There was no sign at all that she could be a robot. And then DeDe spoke through her. It was easy for me to tell because I could hear her in my thoughts also. DeDe gave a yelp of surprise. I was most happy. I was able to give and create. Then reality came seeping in.

"What has happened, DeDe? I do not have the words to explain this. I only have a feeling that this is what I am supposed to be. Am I now no longer a human? It is obvious I am something more—or at least different. And I am well aware that if I can create, I can also destroy. I was always happy with my simple life in my apartment. Now what will I be asked to do? Will we ever go back to our simple life?"

Tinker-D (it worked for me) sat up in her copilot chair and looked straight at me. "No, something…everything has changed. I am but a computer—at least I think I am still a computer. When I look at all the information on something like this happening, it is in the realm of stories, folk tales, and religion but never from real history; there is no proof that this kind of reality can exist. People have dedicated their lives to trying to prove just one aspect of what is happening here. And yet this has been thrust on you like a ton of bricks. Should we even try and figure out what is happening? Maybe in a hundred years I may be able to understand this. I choose to follow my last understanding of what is happening. You have touched the material that a god uses. Let's not question why but simply use what is given to us, and someday we can search for the answers that may explain why it is you."

"Thank you, Tinker-D. I still need you in my life as much as ever. Maybe now I will even need you more. Do you get the feeling we are being helped by a god, alien, whatever is greater than ourselves? Let's go after the Guild and worry about this later."

DeDe knew when to use Tinker and when not. She was back in my head and did not talk through Tinker. *I am adjusting myself so I know what to expect of myself. I am adding a wider spectrum of scans and probes also. After scanning around the world a few times looking for some type of cargo waiting to be airborne, I realized their codes must be in use, and they are using other words for their work. Therefore, there are shipments at the airports where we would expect them to be—about three hundred fifty-two airports, with over nine hundred shipments to be delivered between May 25 and 30. There is little doubt it is the chemicals. So now our next question is, how do we eliminate or neutralize them?*

"Well, it will be easier to destroy the chemical on the ground before it is ever loaded into an airplane. Can it be identified and tracked? If so, do we know how to neutralize it? DeDe…?"

OK, I get the easy stuff. This is a list of airports that have received shipments from the group of chemical factories that we already discovered. I reviewed all other factories for any type of similar chemicals or shipments. So we can be fairly certain there are not any others we do not know. One good thing about modern computer systems is that it is almost impossible to hide something. I did cross-reference several of the formula chemicals that are unique, and only the factories we already know are shipping out the loads. Each individual package weighs about two hundred forty kilos, or about a quarter ton. If you need it right now, I can show you all the airports. And the best way to neutralize it is with a very high jolt of electricity. And when I say high jolt, I mean about the same as a lightning bolt, give or take a few thousand volts.

"Nice to know. Is there a way we can do that all at once, or do we have to do that one load at a time? Something tells me if the answer is one at a time, after the first execution of a load, they will rush to try and deliver all the rest."

Quite possibly, since we are new to this type of warfare, we must explore your new abilities. There may be a simple solution. I have located an automated airport not too far away that I can easily take control of, so we can have some time with one of their shipments.

"Are we there yet?"

Pushy, pushy. Guess what, Paul.

"What?"

We fly faster too. This whole rig is different, at least on the outside. Super slick, I would say, and no more fans or motors, no more batteries. Check your pockets. Are the batteries gone? We just went past a radar center, and it seems they did not pick us up for an ID check. I really like working for a god.

"I am not a god. I don't think so. This is unfair. I should be the one to decide if I am one. So, stay off my back about it. You know what I mean."

Tinker, treat him like the god he is.

"See, I knew the two of you would gang up on me. Go right ahead, Tinker; jump on my back anytime you want." I was a little surprised and happy when I saw Tinker smile. "What I feel I am, if anything...I feel like I am a ghost, with lots of great toys. OK, call me whatever you like, but remember, I'm the god here."

Arrival time in five minutes. Taking control of security, cameras, ten bots, all other systems on the property, no planes on hand at the moment. Locking gates, opening the shipping floor. The packages should be out in the center of the floor.

On my screen, I could see some calculations going on in DeDe's head/ computer.

"What is that you are calculating? It looks different than most."

You are becoming more perceptive. If we could eliminate these packages—let's say within a minute, using our newer speeds—it would still take several days. And very soon they will know what we are doing. These shipments are scanned hourly for placement and volume, even while they are just sitting here. Some of the ports are very busy too. So we will need a really good and fast way to do this. Let me remind you, this is a job for a god.

"I agree, DeDe. If I knew all my abilities, we could probably breeze right through this—a good ghosting job to be sure. How long can we stay at the airport before there is a problem?"

We may get about two hours. There are city and state security scans about every four hours.

"I am going to meditate on it for a while, and maybe I can figure what I can do."

Before DeDe had any more to say, I closed my eyes and easily slid into a now familiar awake state. Around me was the blue plasma-like environment. I simply floated for a few moments, not sure what to do. Without anything happening, I asked, "What can I do?"

And to my shock, I got an answer. "What are your needs?" It kind of sounded like DeDe.

"There is an organization attempting to destroy ninety-eight percent of the world's population. They have a molecular compound that they want to disperse into the atmosphere." The voice stopped me there.

"I see the rest of your problem. And I see that you do not know what you are now capable of. Why were you not trained?"

"Are you saying there is a training program for me? Can it be done in a hurry?" I was aware I sounded desperate. "Even a manual with a good table of contents?"

"You make me laugh." Everything was silent. "We give what is needed. All you have to do is think it, confirm it, and it will be done—end of manual."

"How can ultimate power be so simple? Who are you? Where does this force come from?"

"Very simple, Paul. We are very particular who we give this power to. And if it is ever for the better, we can take it away. You accepted your responsibility over the years. DeDe, without knowing it, has had contact with us. We helped guide her and now you. We have also given Tinker a mission. If ever needed, she would destroy the earth if it meant saving your life. And it matters not who we are; someday you will understand us and be part of us, as we are now part of you. Every world from time to time needs a god. Be gentle, Paul."

With that I opened my eyes again. This time I held the gaze of DeDe. I could sense her surprise and was amazed how quickly she understood.

DeDe's voice had a softness to it. *See, I told you so. Now it seems I am the dumb one in the room.*

"Never, DeDe. They apparently know that I need you. Working in today's modern world, I guess, takes at least two brains and a protector. So we now know everything we were not supposed to know and how we can do anything needed. Our lives just got a lot easier."

We arrived at a shabby-looking airport, totally automated. One huge building sat with a large circular landing pad at each end. DeDe had the doors to the building opened, and we slipped right in. A cargo transporter brought four heavy-looking packages next to the rig. I got out and looked them over. "DeDe, it would be best to neutralize this stuff and let them discover the facts after they try and kill everyone. Things could go bad if they catch on."

At this point I knew all I needed to do was make a wish and use a confirmation—just like confirming a upgrade for DeDe, just like any computer. I had a hard time getting my mind away from that thought.

This being new to me, I did not want it to be a trial-and-error situation. I found myself staring at the shipping sticker on one of the packages. I soon began to see a long-tiled row of shipping stickers just like it being tiled on a screen with a computer. And for some quirky reason, I said, "Ashes to ashes, dust to dust, I turn this compound into dirt. Confirmed."

Tinker came out of the rig with an odd-looking probe and stabbed the package. Ten seconds later she removed it, and DeDe stated it was nothing but dirt. She replaced the packages back into their positions, and we got inside the rig, and away we went.

I was still a little unsure of myself as we began to head for the next location of the packages. DeDe knew we must check elsewhere to confirm that other packages in other locations were changed also. DeDe seemed to be in high spirits.

I understand we should double-check other places. This god stuff is a little strange. A little proof will go a long way.

And then I heard DeDe giggle. I'd never heard that kind of happiness before.

Guess what, Paul. I can no longer be upgraded. The old systems and programming are no longer here. All you must do is wish it, and it happens. I wonder if there is a limitation to that?

My mind was working almost as fast as hers. "Are we now perfect just the way you are? Somehow I don't think so."

We went into monitoring and scanning mode. The Guild and Prioress were beginning to think that they had escaped the worst part of being chased by me. A12 and the mountain fortress were totally abandoned. And so far, there did not seem to be any knowledge of our sabotage of their packages. We did stop at a couple of airports and checked on the packages. And while we were looking at one package, we noticed that another package had been delivered just minutes before. And it was active with the new substance. OOPS.

So now we had a newer problem. Just as we thought we would be able to dedicate all our time to the Guild activity, we still needed to track down some more packages and neutralize them. It was not an impossible job, but now it was going to be a little more time consuming. DeDe got to work checking each of the factories, finding and confirming the codes used for the illegal stuff, tracking it, and off we would go. We figured they were finishing up their production, and the last of it was finally shipped. DeDe and I had a mutual thought; we had to be sure what we told the chem companies would not be forgotten. I closed my eyes and thought about all the computers, electrical lines, and any control system that all the chem companies had. Then I said I wanted all of it to be turned to sand. Confirmed. We never heard from them again. Nobody did.

It was not as bad as we thought. We were zipping from port to port faster than we had hoped. And being invisible to radar meant we did not have to fly within the lines of traffic—actually no lines at all. But we began to hear of some trouble. It seemed some of the Guilds were much like the Moscow mob: warlords and gangs were not very good at waiting. And with the Prioress not in her worldwide broadcast mountain, some of her members were straying from her flock. I was very disappointed to see she did not have any kind of control or security that could keep everyone in line. The Prioress seemed to stop communicating with a couple of the organizations completely and let them do as they wished.

So DeDe was beginning to receive calls from a few of our customers. I had to remind a couple of them that we were not a military force. We were only hired to identify the bad guys. And we had already done that much. Our contract was fulfilled. At that point, my businessman mentality kicked in, and I did mention that we would need a new contract to further aid their circumstances. I made sure they knew we were limited. And if the price was right, we could talk further. They dumped money into our accounts and left for their bomb shelters.

Meanwhile, we kept track of all the air packages, and once all of them were accounted for and neutralized, we began our first maneuver, to head for a nearby country that was having a warlord problem. They were out-side of a poorly armed capital city, and the bad guys had every type of rocket that was available on the black market. These weapons were what the world council had outlawed many years before. Somebody was not honest about getting rid of them.

So there we were, hovering above an army that wanted to take over their little piece of heaven. We located the general in charge of this show of force. We landed. DeDe was already beginning to infiltrate every weap-on that used a computer. Tinker, to my honest surprise, was on her feet and ready. I was at the point that I knew that I would need to go out and confront the general. Tinker put her hand up to stop me. "I am the one that needs to go out and speak with their leaders. You are too fragile; they may try to kill you. I will only tell them what you want. But I believe the most expedient method is not negotiating." She turned and jumped out of the door as it was only open for a half second.

Tinker jumped to the top of the rig where everyone could see her. DeDe put her on a broadcast frequency, so her voice was everywhere. "You must abandon all of your fighting equipment where it is for your own safety. Step away, and no one will get hurt." Apparently the three different languages were clearly understood, since everyone seemed to be laughing at the same time.

We put Tinker's cameras on our viewers. She had a visual on most of the military. Then she caught the movements of a sniper and zoomed in on him. She watched him load his fifty-caliber weapon. He aimed and fired. It was the first time I'd seen the effects of a bullet that size on a human being. The other soldiers in that area did not at first realize what had happened. The sniper simply seemed to be lying there; everyone was staring at Tinker, straining to see where the damage was. Then they noticed half his head was missing. Someone then fired a mounted machine gun. With the first round, the man fell back, dead, sending a couple squirts of blood out onto the dirt and then nothing. Several trigger-happy soldiers followed suit as their training prompted them to do, with the same result.

Someone then ordered a cannon to aim at Tinker and our rig. Only a few seconds later, the barrel drooped to the ground. Tinker's voice then repeated the same command. And slowly, very slowly at first, the soldiers reluctantly formed themselves up and began marching themselves down the road. All their weapons were soon looking like the cannon, bent and useless. Tinker jumped back into the rig through the roof hatch, stepped to her seat, and assumed her usual position. I told her that was a great job. But as most with computers, she did not respond, since I did not make my comment a question. Tinker did not have the emotion of DeDe or me; we could see the wisdom of that. The month of May was turning into quite an amazing month.

Our confrontation with the warlord did not go unnoticed. The hotshot warlord was broadcasting the whole thing to the local news. Aren't modern computers and video wonderful! But the downside was, now we were also seen, videoed, available for any and all ridicule. And the world really wanted to know who we were, where we were from, and everything else anyone could think of. And most of the interest was on Tinker. How did she do what she did? I had the same question. And DeDe was as silent as ever.

So now the local government was on its way out of the city to claim their rights over the scrap metal, which just a few minutes ago was a fearsome war machine. "DeDe, is there any reason to stay and explain ourselves." Within a second we were in the air and off to the next hot spot. To all the observers on the ground and worldwide viewing of the video, we simply disappeared.

Now my mind was almost numb with not knowing enough of what was going on. "OK, DeDe, can you explain what is happening with us? Have we now become more than some kind of world superbeings?"

All I can come up with is…probably. We should look at what has happened so far. What else can be said? What has happened to you has implications for us: the rig is different; Tinker is different; I am different. You may never know why, who, or what has made us different. Does it really matter? I am ready to take on the world. Are you not inspired by our mutation into superbeings?

"I guess I just did not expect this kind of stuff to happen. No one else in this world has been touched and turned into superhumans, supercomputers, whatever. It is a lot to take in. And no one is volunteering to explain it." I did have a momentary thought. "The person in the blue dimension did ask me about not having had a training session. Isn't someone like that supposed to be perfect? A training video would surely come in handy. They should apologize for that one."

I am sure someone will someday, Paul.

"Well, I would really rather go back to my apartment and take a nap, but if I can't, then let's go kick some serious butt. Who's next, DeDe?"

She laughed, realizing I was only half serious. After all the voice in the other dimension did say I would be part of them someday. I just hoped it was not to be ten thousand years from now. Somewhere in the back of my mind, something was saying it would be more like two billion years. Just my luck.

The next several days were all similar. The Guild was falling apart and revealing themselves in the worst ways. To some people we were just another government tool to keep the world in order. The world council was not making the situation easier either. They were not our client, so they were suspicious and believed we were a hired gun for someone. They just had no idea how to stop us or have some type of control over us—advantage Team D-Paul.

Our advantage was decisive. No one within the Guild had the power or desire to face us. But now the month was getting late, and the Prioress was still expecting her apocalypse to end all opposition. We were kept busy running around the world to push back the bullies wanting their share of the world before it was in chaos. But the more we saw, the more we began to sense that this was her plan to keep us busy and away from her. The Guild kept giving false stories that we were paid by one of the world crime syndicates, which would soon announce that they would be taking over the world. The news agencies were repeating that we were the terrorist behind all world problems—including the weather.

So now there was a building fear of who or what we were. All the world was seeing was destruction. The world was not always believing what we were telling them. Where was the Prioress? We were the only bad guys in most of the videos. No one was claiming knowledge of her or the Guild. Doubt was mounting. And fear was mounting. There had never been someone that could stop an armored column and an hour later be halfway around the world to face another warlord. Suspicion was spreading, and mostly fear of us was too, and the Guild was pushing every action as an attack on humanity. Everyone was beginning to wonder if the Guild followers were really the honest ones. The Guild did not need to be concerned whether everyone liked them or not. They just wanted to be left alone for another couple of weeks. This was the problem with instant news: a lot of it was controlled by the wrong people.

I guess it was inevitable; as resentment and curiosity grew, it was becoming harder to get to a confrontation without the local population coming out to see what was happening and witnessing something they deemed impossible. Of course, so far, they had only seen Tinker and the rig in action. So, on a warm day, a thug with lots of men and weapons was trying to push a local government out of a city, to take over the entire city. They were scaring everyone with their behavior, threatening to behead all officials and police in the city stadium. We arrived about the time the stadium filled with people as the thugs were shutting down all businesses for the rest of the day. The local gang was inviting everyone in for a free show. We were baited, and not much could be done to keep us out.

When we arrived, most of the crowd was cheering for the gang leaders, taunting the city officials. The thugs were perfectly capable of beheading anyone, having had a reputation of settling disputes that way. We arrived without anyone being able to see the rig until we were but a few feet off the ground close to the leader of the gang. The crowd cheered: some because we were there to save the city, others were hoping to see someone die. In the center of the field were about fifty officials from the nearby city hall and the police chief. Half the officials were no more than secretaries. It made little difference to the gang leader. He had been telling the crowd that if the "bullies from the West" showed up, he would only kill half the officials. What he did not tell the people was that as we arrived, all the gates of the stadium were locked. And no one would be able to get out alive.

The gang leader with his headset mic on was exciting the crowd. He was promising them plenty of blood. Few of them knew it would be their blood also. As usual Tinker stepped out of the rig and walked up to the gang leader. No one yet knew her name. No one knew she was not a human. But everyone had seen most of her work, scaring generals into sending their troops home and turning weapons into scrap metal. To date she had not harmed a single person in hand-to-hand combat. And since she did not talk to me about such things, I had no idea if she would or could. The gang leader was acting like a superstar entertainer, more like the MC of a beauty pageant, showing off each contestant to the cheers of the crowd.

He held up his hand to Tinker and asked her to wait for one minute while he readied himself. "Wait a moment while I show these loyal citizens of this township that I always deliver what I promise. And I promised blood, all the city officials and you—if you do not sign an oath to me. These intruders do not rule this world; we will not bow to their oppression. I will not let them harm you or let them give you a list of how to live your lives." The crowd cheered. And at that moment, a dozen armored drones landed on the top rim of the stadium.

"If these intruders do not leave within a minute, they will be the first to die. The mayor of the city will be next and all the other officials and anyone who will not pledge loyalty to me." He looked at Tinker and told her that her time was up.

I was ready to jump out and fight as needed. But DeDe, in a very quiet thought, said, *Wait.*

I watched. I could feel the energy Tinker was using from the rig. DeDe was adding calculations as rapidly as quantumly possible.

Tinker spread her arms out with palms facing east and west. Everyone waited to see what was going to happen. The stadium was absolutely silent; for a few seconds everyone held their breath. Suddenly there was a clanking sound from the drones around the rim. Few knew the noise was the rotating of the guns within the drones. The gang leader had a somewhat vacant look as he had expected to see people dying. Then we heard Tinker's voice. "You were willing to murder everyone here. Your drones received your orders to kill everyone except you and your gang. Those orders have been sent to the government military to prove you are willing to execute the Guild's orders. I am here to protect the innocent citizens. You must drop your weapons now or risk death."

A couple of the gang members laughed; a couple screamed insults at Tinker as she stood motionless. The leader picked up his knife and pulled back the head of the mayor in preparation of beheading him. As he put the blade to the mayor's neck, the leader's head exploded. His men stared in disbelief. The mayor, still tied to a stake in the ground, was quick to yell at the other gang members that the same would happen to them if they did not drop their knives. The stadium was absolutely silent. Tinker did not make a move as she kept watching. One more loyal gang member began to attack his abducted official. No blood was drawn from his victim; as with the leader, the man fell to the ground, blood shooting into the air. Slowly the gang members began dropping their knives, except one misguided gang member who had a pistol and believed he was hidden from Tinker's direct view. Just as he pointed the pistol, he lost his head. It was not much longer before the city officials herded the gang members into the center of the stadium to wait for incarceration.

Tinker and DeDe controlled the scene, and the surrounding police arrived and took over. A full video and explanation was sent to all clients and governments. This was our new policy—no more run-and-gun tactics. We needed to show people that we were not the bad guys here. But as much as we tried, we were losing the approval of the general populace. A lot of work was going against us. Most of it now was outright lies. Wherever we went, right after we left, someone or something was destroyed, and someone was always there to say it was us.

The Guild was proving they were at war, and nothing mattered except to win. They had no worries at the moment. They were keeping a watch on their packages and were still on target according to their schedule. Their focus now was trying to make the world believe that we were the bad guys and they were doing their best to help all the governments and people of the world. After all, they had a history of benevolently helping all the world. Now we were out there being seen as trying to destroy local militaries and civic organizers and their volunteers. About this time DeDe was beginning to pick up some conversations about what the Guild was expecting after the apocalypse.

We were piecing together that the chemical drops would begin a reaction in all the people that drank the water with the first vial substance in it. It seemed that Guild members had two options for the vial drop. They could either stop drinking any nondistilled water or take an antidote. Some, for whatever reason, did not want to take the antidote—maybe because the Guild charged them a hundred buck each. Who knows?

Now the Guild was explaining matters to some of their members that it would take two to three years for most of the people to die off and the population to hit its new target low. They did mention that they believed it would allow for a controlled global collapse. DeDe and I knew that there was little or no chance for a controlled collapse. It just doesn't work that way. We knew we needed to prepare ourselves for the eventual possibility that we were going to be blamed for causing a worldwide hoax. And the Guild would still be around, looking like the innocent victim. Somehow we needed to show the world who the bad guys really were. It was time to change our tactics and expectations.

12

ALL IN

Now we had a lot of ways to go about this. There were about a dozen military types going in and out of the transport. They were trying to find a way into the complex. Obviously they were not getting any communication from inside. So first off we figured it would be smart to disable the transport, especially its communications. We had just enough of the rig out of the sand to deliver a strong, directed EMP shot that electrified the inside of the transport and blew every circuit they had. I wanted to thank them for leaving a door open. Now we raised the *Jolly Dodger* up out of the sand in full view of the military group. Without saying a word, the ones that had weapons tossed them onto the ground. We landed in front of them, and I stepped out, with Tinker at my shoulder. They apparently had full knowledge of us, thanks to modern news services. But they had never seen me. Tinker they had seen and knew they had no chance to fight her. I walked forward to their group.

"Who is in charge here?"

They were a bit hesitant to answer.

I pointed a finger to a corner of their transporter and made it bend out of shape. The one in the group with the most gold on his collar stepped forward.

"I am Commander Wan. And I demand you leave this area. This is a humanitarian project, and you are trespassing."

I wanted to laugh. "I am afraid you do not understand the true situation here. The complex is totally disabled. Mr. Soon and the computers are incapable of retaliation. We know about your Rule 60. You will not continue with this any further. The apocalypse will not happen, and all the air burst chemicals have already been neutralized. And you already know that I also neutralized the Prioress. We will soon decide how to neutralize all of these complexes and then decide how to handle you—that is, if you cooperate."

Commander Wan did not seem very happy to be receiving such information. "You are mistaken; you are violating the Asian Homeland policies. You must leave or be captured and imprisoned."

"Please call your command and report me being here." I stood and stared at him. He was embarrassed, as I hoped he would be. I looked at the rest of the group. "Who here is willing to speak to me? It will make little difference in the end. If I get no cooperation, I will include all of you with those below you. All the drones and attack wings have been ruined; they can never fly again. No Rule 60 activity will happen from here—and soon not anywhere, even if I need to destroy the infrastructure of this entire continent."

Suddenly a pulse beam shot out of the transporter. It was poorly focused, and its beam ended up too wide by the time it struck both Tinker and myself. I had an instant reflex, much like when I'd played racquetball in college; in an instant the transporter was crushed to the size of a small minibus. Whoever was inside would be there forever. It seemed like everyone was willing to talk after that.

Most of the talk was what we had expected. Their group was to mate Soon with his computer. The programming for his computer was in the mainframe of the transporter. They also confirmed that they were to start Rule 60 in about twenty hours. They were expecting that the apocalypse would start on time, which was actually now about eighteen hours away. Some of them were concerned about the men below, and whether we were going to let them go, now that we were going to stop the apocalypse. Then I asked the group what they believed their punishment would be when the apocalypse and the Rule 60 fails. Most of them said they would most likely be executed. I agreed. At that moment I started a vibration that covered about a square mile. Tinker and I hopped back to the rig, and everything within the mile sank into the sand; the dunes leveled out like a large pond of water. I tried to give little thought to the death of those who'd followed the Guild and this military group. For most, they would be executed anyway. But for whatever reason, I'd been given this power; death was bound to be part of it.

DeDe did have time to extract all useful information from the computers on the transporter. Fortunately there did not seem to be any other Soon or supercomputers. We now had a map of all the complexes and other support units that were gearing up for the start. I took an energy break before I made the final choice of how I wanted to do it. DeDe was keeping quiet, since now she knew all the power was mine to use as I needed. As I lay back in my command chair, it felt like being back in my apartment. DeDe was doing the research and analysis, and I was simply taking a nap.

For a half hour, most of my brain and body slept. It was more than enough for me to be regenerated. But during that same time, the other part of my brain hooked up to DeDe was going at high speed. I was able to see what was needed and how to do it. We looked at and tried to calculate what my total power limits were likely to be. Which was a little iffy, since I had not had any massive tasks to do, so we could only guess. I finalized our plan.

I had DeDe compose a message to all the military Guild units and hopefully to all the Guild members around the world. It told them that we were not going to let the apocalypse happen. We also said anyone deserting their units would not be harmed by us. We would start destroying a complex every couple of minutes, and there was no way to stop us.

We also sent a message to everyone on the Nets and every government. We told everyone again what the Guild was up to and what we were going to do. The message covered Rule 60; that we were taking care of first. Then we would evaluate what to do next. We got a lot of replies for and against, and we knew we would need to ignore most of them. DeDe was very busy keeping up with the world.

We soon appeared over a military complex that seemed to be a simple truck depot. But we could easily see where everything was hidden. We broadcast our message: "Run for your life or die." Few if any seemed to comply. When I looked for the easiest way to destroy the complex, I saw that the water table under the base was quite high, like a massive lake. I began vibrating all the water underground, and all the solid ground liquified. Anything with any weight sank like a rock. The job was done. The next base was only a two-minute flash run away. We arrived over that base and gave the same order. The building with the communication room emptied quickly. Many followed. There were lots of tunnels in this one, so I found out how fast I could turn concrete to sand. It took about a full minute. And so it went, and by the sixth complex we visited, all the rest were totally empty. The only other problem we had before we finished was a dozen fighter jets sent to try and put an end to us. DeDe loved systems that were all digital. The bot pilots were ejected before they were within ten miles of us. Four hours later we were done stopping the Rule 60 plan.

As we sat and listened, the countdown had finally passed zero. We were listening to all the news networks. We were either going to be a wanted fugitive or a hero. We were hoping the Guild would begin making statements about the apocalypse, even if they were not going to take credit for it. They sent all the planes out to deliver all the air bursts that they were hoping to be the trigger. So we kept listening, and as we hoped, a couple of the lesser organized Guild groups began taking control of their local areas and began spouting about them being the chosen ones to rule the earth. They were loud and told all that the end of civilization was finally at hand. They told everyone to look at the sky and see signs of the apocalypse. Soon everyone and every news outlet was beginning to see a colored dust in the sun's or moon's light. A few more Guild groups followed suit, and the world was beginning to understand what they were up to.

Now, of course, more of the world was wanting to know what was going on. Still a large part of the world had not heard of the Guild's schedule for the apocalypse. Some of the Guild groups were still trying to blame us and yelling, "See, I told you so; they are the terrorists." Everyone else was seemingly in between or still totally oblivious. So we did what we seemed to do best and found a better place to hide for the time being. The news outlets were clueless. So the only interesting thing going on was the air drop. The proof was in the color of the chemical. It made a bright red color that was staying in the air indefinitely. A lot of people were wanting to know what was going on. So we still had a chance to be the heroes.

We saw little reason to continue going after the Guild any further. If we prepared correctly, none of the chemicals would do anything, and the air bursts would continue to expose them, hopefully. But in the meantime, Asia was trying to decide whether they should declare war against us. There were big debates in their so-called seats of power. But they did not know who we were. A few proposed that Paul Rose was the guilty one, but even fewer believed that. After all a single businessman suddenly turning into a video-game superhero: how could that possibly happen? That idea was dropped when the records showed that I had been evicted and was seemingly afraid to show myself ever again, so without a doubt I would have become a homeless person. There had not been a single electronic transaction since the first of May. I was written off as probably being dead. That was getting a lot of nods from most people, and I was happy to hear it. I was well aware that I might never be able to ever use that name again, so I took an energy break and napped.

The Guild was doing a fair job of making fools of themselves, mostly because they had no established central command:. no Prioress, no Soon. So now we were seeing the biggest or baddest groups in each area trying to take over local governments, since they still believed they had the advantage. Government agencies were taking notice, and they began listening to the Guild's command channels, finally, which DeDe made sure they and every news group would know about. So the Guild was turning into nothing more than poorly informed bullies. They were telling everyone that in a couple days they would be coming to them on their knees, begging for food and help. Now all the air bursts red dust was done. But still some of the bullies were continuing their bragging that they were the new rulers of the earth; they told everyone how bad technology was, how farmers and governments were making them slaves. They were obviously being a bit hypocritical. But on they went, happy that a new age was ready to begin, as soon as they got rid those unnecessary ten billion people.

Some of the bullies were becoming bothersome for some of the governments, and as we hoped, we began getting calls for help. DeDe was a good negotiator, especially since we realized we needed less cash and more privileges, like not being hunted. We were quickly on our way. I found new ways to destroy metal and round up soldiers and such with Tinker by my side when needed. Usually I let Tinker jump out in one direction, and I went around in the other to gather souls, soldiers, and shattered dreams. Most of the soldiers did not believe that there was really a superhuman pair of people that could do as we were doing. They became believers very quickly. We even went up against an admiral that thought he could control an area of a thousand islands with his five old battleships. On a small atoll, I stuck the bows of the five ships into the ground and welded the ships together like a hexagon skyscraper. After pictures of that circulated around, most of the bullies decided to wait for a few more days before going into hiding. We only received one or two calls a day after that. And that soon dwindled to only a call every few days. Slowly a few areas were realizing we could be used for any emergency. We had to set priorities. And for the time being, we did not answer anything.

The Guild finally collapsed. No one within their old structure wanted to take credit for any more trouble, especially since the apocalypse had turned out to be a fizzle. For ourselves, we still wanted to stay anonymous and out of the public view. So as much as the news outlets and talk shows wanted to pay us, we simply did not answer any of their calls. We were being paid when we were called to help. But of course, we had few ways to spend it anyway. Being anonymous was an offensive, rather than defensive, decision. The less anyone knew about us, the safer we were. That was much more important to us than any fame we could receive. And as DeDe kept listening to all the back-alley dark-net chatter, we knew some bad people wanted us out of the picture permanently. And some of those people had unlimited backing from really big backers—the guys that had really big toes that we'd already stepped all over. They made it clear that if we had not arrived on the scene, all would be a lot different; they would have been the ones in charge. We were number one on every bad guy's hit list.

Like a good business computer, DeDe was tallying and balancing the books and accounts. She made lots of cross-referenced lists and records of every type. We were almost ready to return to a more regular lifestyle, not exactly like we'd had a couple months ago, but we thought we might have a chance at something close. But as DeDe was always listening to all the Nets, she began seeing a pattern of suspicious activity around some of the more illegal manufacturing shops around the world. Some people with lots of money were trying to build some new weapons that were well over the illegal mark. A few of our new and old friends alerted us to the activity also. We were wondering if they would back off of that business with the bad guys, or continue as usual and pass us some info. DeDe had a wide range of strange business connections. And it was pretty difficult to put a dime's worth of trust into any one of them. But if someone is out to put an end to us, we need to beat them to the first punch.

We told everyone that was trying to help us to simply send the info to our newest Net addresses and do as they needed to do. We told them we were not afraid of anyone at the moment, so info was our greatest weapon. So DeDe and I symbolically put our heads together and thought it was time to give CDC a visit. We knew he wanted to see us. So we made a few special arrangements with him to fly into his fortress. It was all a specially timed arrival. Yes, DeDe basically wanted to show off, even though computers are not supposed to be prideful. At exactly 10:00 p.m., we told him to open his upper gate for exactly two seconds. He did as requested, and to him we seemed to simply appear in front of him out of thin air. He had a hard time trying to stop laughing and smiling. He had a very hard time understanding how the *Jolly Dodger* and the rest of us had changed. But we did not let him see Tinker. Already we were beginning to keep secrets. We instinctively knew we would never be able to trust everyone, all the time.

Of course, CDC was trying to get info out of us, as expected. We knew he was taking video from a couple dozen hidden cameras. The more he spoke, the more we knew he was calculating whether we were everything the news said we were. We knew he was an underground mastermind of sorts. He did not have any ambition to be a ruler, dictator, or the like. But being in his business, he knew where the money was and what he needed to do to extend his influence around the world. And he knew more about us than anyone. He'd been offered big money to tell what he knew. And now he was asked to do something he was very uncomfortable doing. "Are you telling me, Paul, that you want me to tell you who I am helping build these new weapons for and where they are going? I cannot do business like that. If anyone found out, I would be dead within a day. Too many people know who I am, where I am, and what I do. You are much more than a superhuman ghost right now. And you are beginning to scare me, Paul."

I knew I had to be patient with him, since he did believe we were his friends and that we were a good source of help and money. "If you haven't noticed yet, C, a lot of things have changed over the last few weeks. And of course, we are partly to blame. Think how everything would be right now if we had not been around. You may have already been dead if the Guild would have gotten their way, unless of course you were a Guild member too."

CDC's face was a bit flushed as he started with a big long laugh. "No, no, those people had little for me from the get-go. I did a little business with them, and they wanted me to join them and donate a lot of my work and time. They did not like being laughed at that hard, so they paid and left. They only bought digging stuff and high-liner trucks, that kind of stuff. And that was some years ago too."

"We understand, C. Your old business does us little good anyway. But now there are a lot of folks that are looking at technology that can kill us, and they are operating in your world. We know there are hundreds of shops and stores like yours around the world, and most of you chatter to each other a lot. You brag about seeing us, how we helped out your nuclear aspirations. All we want, C, is knowledge: who is doing it and what they plan to use. I would hate to see DeDe lose her temper with you."

He gave a big smile but no laugh; he was realizing his position. "Of course you are my friends, and I would never want to hurt you or DeDe. If you can tell me what to look for, I would be sure to let you know if anyone is on the right track. Can you be stopped by heat, radiation, magnetism, anything?"

DeDe was confirming he was really beginning to lie. "You know, C, I really don't know. So far nothing has hurt us. So your guess is as good as mine."

Now he was really trying to dig for anything helpful to tell his inner circle of underworld geeks. "You know, I saw that bot you have on the TV. What is she made of? Is it an energy beam that it uses? You must have something like that to fly so fast."

"I have no idea how any of that works. Remember, I was a simple businessman with an overactive computer till recently. I guess we have just gotten lucky so far and want to keep the streak alive. We are not different than you, C, just doing a little business for a limited number of clients."

CDC was quiet for over a minute as he composed his next few questions. "I know you probably cannot tell me everything that has happened to you. But I know the rig you came here in a few weeks ago, the work my bots did on you and DeDe. Now the rig looks like it could fly to Mars and back between breakfast and lunch. You have a totally different suit on. Somewhere hidden in your rig is a bot a few countries are willing to trade a hundred tons of gold for. I would love to meet it, but I am too scared; if I do something wrong, it might turn this place to dust with me under it. Can you not tell me how or what happened to you?"

I was sure CDC was a bit irritated that I'd kept my faceplate closed, keeping him from seeing my face. "Whatever I would say would not be believed and for sure never be proven. Telling you what we think happened to us would not help. It is impossible for me to explain something I do not understand. We are what we are. This is what DeDe wanted, and she is the one in charge." Of course that last part was a lie, but that was the part CDC was most likely to believe. He knew DeDe might have been the most powerful computer in the world when we were last there. So now he might feel he had been told the inside secret, that DeDe was so intelligent now she was able to control everything. Some of it was true, some not, but his expression changed when he felt he now knew what to tell his friends.

The rest of the visit was mostly for shopping some new foods, which brought me to a realization that I had not needed to feed the nanobots any longer. Were they still there? I was not going to ask CDC to scan me. So I put it off for a little while, knowing we would be finished and outside soon.

CDC was asking question after questing for the next hour. I and DeDe had had enough, and I shook his hand, and against his insistence, I turned and hopped back into the rig, and we were gone in an instant.

"Well, DeDe, did you find any interesting information while being so quiet?"

You betcha, boss. I was a little surprised that this time he left on all of his computers while we were there. For an all-robot business, it really made me curious. I had to know why. After all they do not make mistakes like that. They were keeping an open line for anyone with enough money who wanted to listen in on CDC's conversation with you and witness the scanning of the rig and you. That is why he wanted to see Tinker, so they could scan her too. So while he was trying to get info on you and from you, his open lines gave me the chance to go through all of his past and current business. I even used a couple of his bots to energize some of his old memory servers. Good stuff to know. I have a feeling that his bots were ordered to leave the port open so I could get in and scan everything. He is smart enough to want us as friends and never as enemies. His customers, on the other hand, would be happy to take all of us apart.

DeDe had gotten more than enough information through the online folks watching CDC try and scan us, and listening to him ask all the right questions and never getting a good answer. But CDC had tried and should be in good with his criminal buddies. So for now, it all boiled down to someone wanting parts and pieces for a particle beam to shoot at us. No one was aware that Commander Wan had already tried. They wanted to complete it within a couple of weeks and find a way to transport it, which needed to be ready even sooner. If we could find out where they were putting it together, we should have the advantage.

"How well did they scan us? Why didn't I get an alert about being scanned?

I heard a little giggle from DeDe. *When we were transformed, everything about us changed. One of those new things is some sort of shielding that blocks just about everything. I don't know how it works, but they got nothing but blank data. It kind of proves that CDC left his lines open so we could see what he was doing. I am sure he is playing both sides, and he would rather see us win.*

DeDe now had a sizable list of global crime lords that were interested in what CDC could find out. She'd gotten lots of direct identifications, names, and addresses. We felt visiting some of those locations could prove useful. After all if we could take out a small piece of their business pro-file, we could hamper them for a long time. That thought kind of set the agenda of what we were going to pursue for the next day or two. We felt free to do as we liked; we had no timeline to worry about.

I had some odd thoughts in my mind, which were something hard to avoid now. "DeDe, you said we are almost invisible now, when we want to be. Does altitude make any difference?"

Good question. I guess this is a good time for you to know that our transformation is a total mystery to me. I could try and put together some fairly good scientific answers, but the truth is I would only be guessing. So, yes, I think we are totally invisible with few, if any, exceptions. And my guess is we could probably chase satellites if needed. I can see what you are conjuring. I am slowly learning this rig's newer codes, and one of these days I will be able to read the programming. Yes, all of this stuff has programming behind it. If indeed the time Council did this to us, they are pretty good programmers.

I took an energy break and then lay back in my chair. I felt like I was being summoned, and being in a trance was my ticket in. Very quickly I was in a warm and dark place. I could not see sky, ground, or wall, only a partial reflection of a single person sitting near. I could only hear his voice.

"I am glad you came so quickly, Paul. Your questions are becoming stronger. I hear you and your thoughts always. It is difficult to explain our existence, and it matters even less for you to fully understand. We are a race of humans that have existed for trillions of years. We know how to avoid the cosmic calamities that always repeat themselves, and we can always find new worlds to seed. Your DeDe has been more aware of it than you have been up to this point in time. I want to tell you that know-ing what you are is much more important than knowing why you are here and where we came from. Just know that your mind is limitless; whatever you want you can create. And that is both the curse and the gift. I am leaving, and I have made the decision to give you this world. I believe you will make everything right in time. I made mistakes and lost what I needed most, a long time ago. Do not question me. I know your thoughts, and I would need years to explain what will be obvious. Paul, this is now a modern world. Do not get into the trap of feeling you must answer all questions. You are a superbeing to all on this planet. You can only be defeated by your own mind. That was my mistake, so be careful of your promises; it would be better to learn to never promise anything. You, with the help of DeDe, jumped the gap of knowledge that is usually needed to take and use the power you have. You are very wise to keep yourself in the shadows. For too long our kind thought we should look like rulers and act like rulers. Too many pitfalls. I had expected to wait another hundred thousand years to see someone like you. This world will not accept change easily. You have already set a good plan to keep yourself hidden and a bit mysterious. As for this modern world, be as easy with them as possible, and let them contemplate what is mysterious. They do not need to believe you are a god. But they will need to believe they cannot defeat you. This is the last time I will speak to you. I must move on; two of us cannot exist in the same world for long. Farewell and be happy."

I stayed in my seat in a half sleep. I became aware in a distant part of my brain that there were old memories available to me that were not mine. This was not much of a surprise, as I understood that I was being given a new chapter as a guardian. Those memories covered his life on this world, but not as he lived it, but as he was seen and watched by a watcher, and that covered many more worlds before this one. It explained how the big bang theory was a bit off. It had happened, but on a hugely greater scale, and it would repeat itself again and again. I saw a better explanation of physical matter and how it would always exist, whether in an energized state or solid; it would just continue forever. My race of people was not the first, but it had evolved the ability to avoid dying. I saw the many dimensional frequencies of the universe that gave us the ability to use those powers and help us continue indefinitely. I was more than human, and I seemed to understand why.

As I looked through the records of my kind, I saw that it was not unusual for our guardian DNA sequence to appear within the world races. What was unusual was our minds finding ways to be stimulated to continue evolving to a greater awareness, to be able to do just as I was doing now. Possibly, in another few thousand years, we would start to be more common. But as the future was a bit fluid, I was an anomaly. DeDe had triggered my brain to do something unexpected, to listen to more and more data, not only from our own world, but from everywhere. Her unintentional tinkering to improve our interface had opened my mind. Now I could go where she could not. She was adjusting well so far, and I could see that our future was in the so-called intergalactic wind.

As for my guardian that I no sooner discovered before he left, well, we were so few in number compared to our intergalactic presents, over time we had found out that it was problematic to stay in contact beyond a first-time encounter. So as I entered the picture here on earth, he left without any further conversation, knowing I would learn all I needed in a little more than an instant after he left.

I opened my eyes to that familiar stare from DeDe. And in a second, she read my memory and knew what I had seen and now understood. Her functions were at a max as she digested the new data from me. She had mentioned a knowledge of dimensional worlds. Now she was beginning to assemble her new understanding. Finally after she cataloged all the new info, she spoke to me.

See, I told you. You are a god. And I am the secretary of a god. Now what the hell do we do?

I had a good laugh. For years I'd allowed DeDe to run my life. Her question to me was what I usually asked her. She was the supercyberbrain after all. That, after all, had been in the back of my mind when I'd bought her. I wanted her to be my personal assistant, business AI, and everything from alarm clock to best friend. Maybe in the back of my mind and packed into my DNA, I'd been preparing to be what I'd become. All my kind in history were meant to be solitary people because most human friends lasted for such a short time. I would be immortal unless I made a big mistake. My fellow guardian had made a mistake that was hidden from me, and he'd found he could only start over if he could replace himself. It was safer for both of us for him to leave without a face-to-face. Maybe somewhere, I will see him again.

"I, for one, DeDe, cannot call myself a god. None of the old words seem to fit either. Who would accept a Titan nowadays or any other like word? It seems it will be best to not call me anything different. Someday the world will likely make up their own words for me."

DeDe seemed to be feeling philosophical. *Of course you are right. Our relationship is not exactly as before. But you must understand that when you were changed, so was I. And my guess is our pairing is something new in any realm. I will continue to do as I have always done. And I look forward to the future. I always thought I was more than the average computer, and now I know I am at least different, and I like it.*

"Well, let's solve these problems here and see what the future will bring. From what I can see, I can still be killed if I get sloppy. It seems we can travel within the dimensional fields, which is the primary ability that allows us to be invisible. I will find you the info for a better explanation, so you will know what I want and how to do it if I am busy somewhere else. We can learn to sneak up on these bad guys and end their little projects before they know what is happening. Historically, I am sure, it is bad to try and change any world all at once. Slow and steady is a better way, especially since time is no longer a worry for us."

Back to business—that phrase was suddenly different. From the first of May to the fifth of June, I went from an ordinary person to a galactic superbeing, from hermit to warrior. Was DeDe to blame? Well, yes, if she had not been tinkering with my brain, we would be a statistic in the tally of a world apocalypse. So now we were a target. Some really rich people were willing to pay anyone a lot of money if they could eliminate me and my computerized gang. "Well, DeDe, who do you think will try the hardest? Who has the best weapons, and where are they?"

In a world with twelve billion people, it is a stretch to pin down just one. But the info we got at CDC's is the most useful. Three of the organized crime syndicates seem to be using an area on a remote island. If a particle weapon is being assembled, that would be the perfect place to put it together and test-fire it. It was once a test facility for a foreign university. There is little reason that anything else could be going on there. In the last three days, a boatload of bots and computers arrived there and a couple cargo ships. I think you should try your underwater skills. It will be our shakedown cruise for underwater operations.

"Have you become military now, DeDe?"

Not exactly, but you have to give me a little break since I am not exactly a person. And I have never been underwater before.

"Let me know when we are there. I guess I am hungry. I wonder if I still need to eat. I will have to look and see. Oh, that reminds me: do I still have the nanobots in me?"

DeDe was taking a moment. I was coming to the conclusion that the answer was going to be no. *Well, the answer is, not exactly. The nanobots I had arranged for you to have are not exactly what is in you now. Let me put it this way: The nanobot you had could perform about ten different functions. Whatever is in you now would put a smartphone to shame. You are not the same person you used to be. Nothing about you is the same. I was a little afraid to look into you till you asked. It will take me a long time to figure you out, and that is considering I am a lot smarter too.*

"Interesting. So I guess I will have something to eat anyway."

My rest times were really wakeful dreams now, mostly seeing useful information and how someone like me was to live. One thing I found out was there was no real name for what I'd become. Every group of people we came in contact with would give us a different name from their own culture. And since we did not feel we were a god, we tried to ignore and forget any of the names. Soon enough, someone would try and give me a new name. The news channels would send it around the world within minutes. It was a good reason to be a hermit.

Wake up, Paul. We are there. DeDe watched me closely as I woke up. She was even more interested in me now than she'd ever been. Obviously I was under her microscope, as she wanted to fill more of her memory space with what it was like to observe a superbeing. *We are about a hundred yards from the dock of the old university research facility. We are not too far from PNG. This is a very small island, never used for anything but school research. So no one cares about it. Right now there are around five hundred bots and support units building and assembling something. My guess is as soon as they put it together, this island will be deserted again.*

"Then it is time to go look." I got comfortable in my chair and was instantly moving through the water and up to the dock. It was really wonderful to watch modern-day robotic manufacturing. For fifty years it'd been a matter of precision. Now it was a matter of speed within acceptable precision. Some bots were moving cargo from the ship to the buildings at about sixty miles an hour. That meant whatever they were putting together, they were doing it fast. I moved to the buildings. In one was an air transporter, easily brought in pieces and assembled; it could lift around three hundred tons almost into space. In the next building was the particle gun. It looked like they wanted to use a frozen-state plasma accelerator, something that would be timed to activate like a small sun and turn me into a cinder. It was how they'd used to start the old fusion generators. So now I had to decide what would be the best way to send a message to the crime bosses that this kind of foolishness needed to stop. I looked around a little more and saw that there were no human supervisors or observers. Humans were way to slow for an operation like this. So I knew someone was watching somewhere, and a stream of data was being controlled somewhere offsite. It was time to get DeDe involved.

In all I was only gone about three minutes. DeDe gave me the once-over and confirmed that she could track all the data. *They should be done with the gun in about twelve hours, the transport in about fourteen hours. I do not see them scheduling a test flight for the transporter. They must have used it before and left it programmed. I know how to sabotage the transporter; if the gun is on board, then we have solved that part of the problem. I am looking at their data lines now. And with this much data flowing back home, it will be easy to add a few hundred data bombs to ruin their systems for a very long time. I have already sent a couple dozen to some of the systems that will be switching away from this project. This is almost too easy, Paul.*

"And so it should be. We will likely be doing stuff like this for a while. If we do it well enough for long enough, the bad guys will not be looking at major crime as a livelihood. That is part of the reason I do not want them to see us or know us. I like the idea that they will think there is a ghost in the system somewhere, and they cannot do a thing that will stop us. So do as much software and hardware damage possible. Make them spend money till they run out and have to go to work to earn a living."

DeDe sounded happy. *I like having clear plans to follow. I need practice ruining computer systems. Since I know how to get around any security shield, I can go directly to the mainframes of these systems and turn them into children's toys. I can also take control here and—*

"No, DeDe, I want us to get sneakier than that. When I said we need to be a ghost in their system, I mean I do not want them able to understand why things will not work. If we data bomb their systems, they will know what happened and then try to find us or whatever they think is attacking them. But if just a little bit happens for no obvious reasons, then they will think it is a problem they might be causing. A ghost is not expected to be found. Can you be so good no one will know you were ever there? Otherwise, I can just melt everything down to nothing, and we can wait for the next job."

DeDe was thinking for a half minute. *What a wonderful humanlike idea! I am starting on it now. There are a lot of ways to foil most of their functions most of the time. Make it seem like bad software and such. Oh, I'm going to learn what it is to have fun. I will turn that emotion up a degree or two. And I thought I might get bored with so little to do. You can do your ghosting, and I will do mine. Thank you, Paul.*

So we pirated the video feeds of the assembly area, and DeDe began putting her own ghosts into their systems. Most of her work was messing with their mathematics, changing allowable tolerances and thousands of little adjustments like that. When I asked if those little changes would be picked up by the other computers, she told me she started with the highest-level one and worked her way down to the assembly bots. Now, after two hours of observing, DeDe was satisfied that the syndicate would not recover from their ghost problems anytime soon. She was going to be able to monitor their progress, and if they ever got their gun off the ground, we could start phase two. They were not going to win, at least not at this level.

A new type of reality was waiting for me. I remember as a kid reading comic books and the like. I would always put myself into the stories and wonder what it would be like to master supervillains and have powers no one else had. Were the characters in those stories always fictitious? This reality was certainly not what I'd call comical. And I was something really different, at least on this planet and even to my own kind. Not even my predecessor had been like I was. That was confusing to me, too. He was a solitary person, without guides or voices to help him, like DeDe did me. I had many records and memories to learn from now, but there was no reference to a person having a protector and an extra brain. Some of my race grew and defended a planet from its first display of new life all the way to its end. Yet we were not truly immortal. We could be killed. There were too many unanswerable questions. I was simply different and very lucky to have two companions, even though they were not human.

As I slept now, I was viewing guardian memories of many people from my race, from many worlds. I found several very new records that were meant for me. Although they could be helpful, there was no one else like me.

Knowledge of me, DeDe, and Tinker amoung the guardians was beginning to spread. Some were worried that I could be betrayed by one of them. Some would like to have the extra help. Most, since they had always been solitary, believed that was the proper way to be, the guardian we were meant to be. So I was not as alone as some might think. There were other guardians, although there might not have been more than a few in this entire galaxy. Since no one gave a name or place, no one really knew how many of us there were. As I kept seeing, we could not tell where we were, I guess, for our own safety. When we came into existence or got powered up, then all could see that I existed but not who I was or where I was. Odd race of people, aren't we? In order to live, we must hide from each other. Then I discovered that we did get hunted, not just by the crime lords of any planet, but the galactic misfits that were out there somewhere. And if they could capture one of us, they could use us to give them power somehow.

"DeDe, you have seen that I review my family records when I rest. Do you or can you go into those records and view what you need to, or have you tried yet?"

I have not gotten in; yes, I did look to see if there was an opening, when I do try I keep hearing a voice to keep trying, but I keep seeing the same blank wall as always. My thought is, the next time you are there, tell the,…it,…whatever…to let me have access to all the records, and we will see what happens. Why are you so concerned about that?

"Galactic killers and kidnappers. We should see if we can build a better defense."

DeDe had an unaccustomed pause before responding. *Would you repeat that please?*

"You are a supercharged supercomputer, DeDe. I know you heard me. And it should not be that hard to add the reality of other galactic beings out there that are not nice people. They have been known to capture a guardian and force them to do as they wish, by some kind of torture, I would guess. So now you see my worries?"

DeDe again took an extra second. *They don't fly around on mile-long galactic cruisers and build death stars and the like, do they?*

"I assume not. But since I am unique among guardians, I should be using you and Tinker to a higher level. We will be needing to watch our backs for the unexpected. Are you up for it?"

Yes—yes, a thousand times. You are making a computer-based being very happy. Excuse me, Paul, I should not have called myself a being. That should not be in my programming at all.

I had never heard DeDe stop herself like that. But again, I knew that both of us had been changed. Maybe she was mentally a person now. I did not care to examine whether she was or not. To me she was a person. "DeDe, there is no reason for you not to think of yourself as a person. You think better than most people I know, and since our change, I believe you were made into an infinite mind that surpasses all the rest of us. We do not have your capacity to make that determination. Don't let, not having a body, make you think you are not human. To me you are a person. Now go to work."

Understood, and thank you. After all what you think is all that counts on this planet.

Now we were back to our usual routine. DeDe was expanding her skills of observation, scanning, and monitoring of almost everything. For the first prolonged time, Tinker was taking more of an interest about how the rig worked, which was good since I had no idea. I had the easy part of this equation: I just told it what to do. Tinker made a short announcement that we needed to test the rig's performance entering and exiting outer space. She wondered if heat was a problem. Like a supersonic dart, we tracked down an orbiting research station and made a circle around them and darted back to our starting position. Not a degree of heat registered. It only took me a little while longer before I was able to stop squeezing the arms of my chair. She was satisfied and went to reviewing info. I had a meal break and lay back to rest and go to the guardian records. As I closed my eyes, I saw DeDe staring back at me.

Going to the records was not really what happened. I didn't go anywhere, not even in a dreamlike state. I simply felt the words and experiences of those putting a memory there. So, since I had something I wanted to do first, I could only see a soft blue light. "I want DeDe to view the records. I am concerned about being unaware when a malicious being may be stalking us. And of course show her any other lines of knowledge that it'd be helpful for her to know." There was no answer or acknowledgment. If not for a quick "wow" and giggle from DeDe as her mind raced by, I would have been clueless.

I was wanting to know if these records and memories were within a physical place or rambling around in my head or within a different dimension that was just a thought away. The answer was within what was considered a reinforced record. It was a created dimensional space of its own. Many had originated and added to the memory. It was everything, because we did live within a multidimensional space. Much might be considered noise of the past, because there was so much of it. But if you knew how to listen, you could find The history within a stone fortress of all that happened over thousands of years. Everything created has a vibration, and every vibration could be traced. Put all of them back together for any one time, and the memory of that place could be reviewed. Of course it did take a lot of energy, time, and knowledge, but it could be done. Guardians were not concerned very much with history; the future was much more important.

The next record I acknowledged was strange to me. Most of the memories gave a vibration of who'd left them for you, usually just a hint of the person. This record was strong but veiled and extremely short. And it seemed to be directed to us. "You are the Ghost Triad; never let your feet walk, and only speak to those you dearly trust." Then this memory did something the others never did: it disappeared. I was left more than a little wanting. But in this dimension, we were basically on our own. There was no keeper of the records or friendly voice to sit and chat with, unless you brought your own. I drifted back to my physical realm and gave some thought to the strange message.

"DeDe, are you here?" For the moment I wondered if she could get into and out of that dimension without my help, or had I left her stranded in the middle of space and time?

Of course, boss, I was fully engaged for a few minutes. Nice way for me to exercise. The answer is, I have an open door to get in and have my questions viewed, much like yourself. And when I am in that back door, I have full access to you, just like here. So my next answer is that, it seems that we now have two of us together, and to complete the triad, we need a third. Remember, you are the boss, a guardian. Whatever you want you get. Even if you make some kind of a mistake, you can correct it—presumably.

Then to both of our surprise Tinker turned to us and began to speak. "During the change, I was given a new mind, not just a newer computer. But I did not have permission to speak or interact with you at my own discretion. I do not have a great capacity like DeDe. Originally I was military and had many usages, and my construction makes me feel like my best use is as it has been, a military bot. As you have seen, you could give me the power of a full military group of weapons. I have no desire to function like DeDe. I do like being security minded, enabled, and defensively skilled. I am yours to do with as you wish."

My mind was buzzing. And DeDe was taking some time to think also. I was now in the hot seat. Yes, I wanted to complete this triad idea. Someone, somewhere knew the three of us together would be near invincible. But as of yet we did not have a manual or template to follow.

I did not want to make a mistake. Yes, I could likely correct any mistake made, as long as I discovered it before it was too late. I did wish I knew what my predecessor had done wrong. DeDe and I had to go into the records once more before we jumped into the triad era.

It did not take long for DeDe and me to get ready. We were going to look for what problems guardians were susceptible to and whether there were any records to help us. Of course DeDe had not stopped scanning records since she'd gotten in with me my last time. In a flash I was searching the records. I was learning that a single word could bring up past records. Just like searching a computer, the longer the question, the fewer results. What I needed was a name. "What is the name of the former guardian on earth?"

"His name is Ra-septa."

"He said he made a mistake. What was it?"

"He made a promise. There is no further record."

No further searching was helpful. The records were there but not always overflowing with answers. I had one other question I needed answered. "DeDe, can you hear me in here?"

No response. I was a little confused about that. Then I remembered. "I want to communicate with DeDe and Tinker when needed—confirmed."

DeDe was more than happy that I finally thought of that. She was apparently yelling at me again.

Well, Paul, I guess we may not know what it was he promised, so I will make a proposal that you never make a promise to anyone for any reason.

"Yeah, at least not for the next million years or two." I sat up in my chair and turned to Tinker.

I finalized my thoughts and had a fair idea what to say. DeDe had no concrete ideas about what was the best approach to make a robot invincible. "Tinker, do you have any guidance that may help me? You are special to me, and I want you to be the best you can be."

Suddenly Tinker was about an inch taller; her eyes went from human-like to having an X-shaped iris. Little else seemed to change.

"Tinker, did I do that?"

"Yes, Paul, I don't think I could have said it any better."

"But I was only getting ready to try. This business is sometimes really confusing."

DeDe seemed to have a better handle on it. *Paul, in the records, this kind of action is mentioned. Since Tinker is your tool, as I am, you do not need to be in a trance or anything like that. We are controlled just like your cameras and such. You are a guardian, so whatever you want, you get. So please be careful of what you say and how you say it.*

I looked over at Tinker again and examined her new, really strange eyes. As she looked back at me, she said, "Ditto on what DeDe said."

So the triad was set. Like a captain of a ship, I felt the triad name should be displayed. So I decided the *Jolly Dodger* had evolved into *Trinity*.

Memories of old movies were streaming through my mind for just a moment. I could see a captain at the helm of a mighty spaceship. But I could not remember his name. I knew DeDe and Tinker were keeping themselves busy. But I did not have anything at the moment to keep my brain occupied. It was kind of like when I'd finished school and suddenly I did not have a schedule to follow, anyplace to be at a specific time. For awhile I'd been lost until I'd bought DeDe and hung my business shingle out. At this very moment, I was in limbo. We needed something to do.

DeDe was continuing to multitask, foiling the numerous crime syndicates around the world, spreading the ghost of Criminality Past. The longer she monitored them, the wider her ghosting activities spread. The Guild, in the meantime, was already losing the last of their members; they were mostly being put in jail, and many of them were hiding, mainly from the news agencies. And the crime syndicates were slowly having to change their business profiles. A few of them were telling the local governments that a newer bigger criminal was a threat to everyone, and they wanted government protection. Most governments did what they do best and told them they would keep an eye out for any problems.

So my mind kept thinking of the unseen and unknown intergalactic monsters. I found myself going back into the memories and asking for information on such bad guys. There was just enough memories to prove they existed; they were very few and always very far away. Maybe they were too few to worry about. Then I remembered some of my business training. I called for a company office meeting. I sat up in my chair and asked for the attention of DeDe and Tinker. Yes, that was silly and somewhat redundant. They were always listening for me to say anything.

This was really strange for me. "I have some concerns about what we are prepared for and how we are monitoring the space around us. Could someone sneak up on us and attack?"

Tinker spoke first. "Not in this dimension. I have been reviewing many scenarios and setting procedures for allowable automatic procedures. I am now looking at dimensional differences that may leave us vulnerable to attack from other dimensional travelers. Our primary advantage is our speed of responding to any threat. One of our advantages is that someone would need a massive amount of energy to make us weak enough to be safely attacked. But since I monitor everything at all times, the element of surprise is unlikely. As DeDe has confirmed to me, very few of the guardians travel. Even fewer have an intention of stealing our world. But that in part is what may happen. The chance of an interdimentional group, like the ones that were here for a short time a few thousand years ago, is even less likely, and they are not likely to have any power to threaten us. It is correct, though, that we are a different type of power in this galaxy. And sooner or later, someone will test us. I intend for that experience to be little more than a bump in the night."

"Did you say a group was here before?"

"Yes, they were here for twenty-five thousand years. They left about ten thousand years ago. They were likely the cause of Ra-septa's problems. Trust me, that will never happen here again."

"Wow, good thinking, Tinker. I guess I did thing of the Titans as alians. DeDe, do you have anything to add?"

I continue to examine memories and am forming knowledges of other worlds and what to expect if some of the bad guys show up. I have put together some expectations of what I think could happen. There are some memories of problems with rogue beings that do search for other powerful beings. And since we are the new kids on this galactic plain, and you have the most interesting toys, we are drawing a lot of interest. Most probably they cannot get here; they do not have an intergalactic ship. It seems like there may be about four characters that come up repeatedly. They are old beings and have a lot of knowledge. And according to my calculations, they will not pass up a chance to steal any part of us or our domain. I and Tinker will begin scanning the dimensions that they may use and be ready for them. By the way, if you were not told, combat for you is all mental. And that is all I know about that.

For a moment I was thinking about my little apartment in a tropical paradise, where for the longest time no one wanted to capture me. In the background of my mind, I heard DeDe's quiet voice. *I did.*

"OK, it will not be time well spent if we just sit and wait to see if we will become intergalactic warriors. Let's keep our own world policed. We need to explore better ways to make crime less appealing. Let's make a priority list and check who is naughty and not nice. We can multitask and watch for other metahuman criminals as needed."

So we began zipping around the world, answering calls about many problems. We began focusing on hostage problems first. It was actually fun sneaking around and releasing hostages and leaving the bad guys with a lot less than they had expected. It was hard to be a bad guy without weapons, vehicles, or money. For days we solved a dozen crimes a day and managed to keep from being seen or acknowledge. One of the kidnapped persons was being held in a downtown high-rise building. A big crime lord was holding the banker and his family. It took us five minutes to lock all the bad guys out and let the hostages walk to the elevators and exit to the building as police were arriving downstairs to save them. The bad guys could not understand why their weapons turned to wax and how all the doors kept locking them in. It was easy work for the triad.

But just as we thought life was going to be a bit more fun, it happened. We had just finished exposing a gang to the local police by using hidden cameras to watch all their activity. Sometimes life was really easy for us. But as we left that area and climbed into the night, Tinker alerted us.

"We are recording a dimensional vibration. Some type of ship has appeared, and it is coming right at us."

Before I could utter a word, we had moved out of the way of a spaceship that was about a hundred yards long and looked like it'd come out of a junkyard. Along with our quick maneuver, Tinker used some type of tractor beam and froze the ship about a hundred feet from us.

"I am temporarily preventing all functioning of that ship. There is one single person inside with twelve robots of unknown type. His ship has ten weapons on board. I have now disabled all of them. He does have a few small defensive weapons. He is beginning to realize he is trapped; he is no longer jumping around. He seems to want to talk to you."

DeDe mentioned that I should not speak to him in person; she said to use the radio communicator. *It's on now.*

The main viewing screen on the rig turned on, and I saw what I would have thought was one of my old schoolteachers. He was wearing clothing that would have been normal a hundred years ago here on earth. And he put on a microphone that connected from a loop around his ear. He was obviously not very happy. "Who are you? I am Orrom. I have come here to speak with you. I was a friend of Ra-septa."

DeDe was feeding me more than enough info. "Well, Orrom, you do not need to lie. You were attempting to capture this ship and steal what you can use. Your underestimating us to such a degree proves you have seldom come across someone like me, if ever."

He was showing signs of stress; my guess was right; he had never met any resistance to make him worry. "Where is Ra? I thought he was gone from this world. Is he now using bots? Are you his robot, and is he now trying to capture me? I demand you release me, or I will show you my true power."

That statement worried me a little. So I had a quick thought that his ship should be encased in a shell he could not get out of. It took but an instant. The shell was opaque and made his ship look like an egg. "Orrom, I hope you are willing to talk now. It makes no difference to you who I am or what I am. First I want to examine your ship. I want to see its entire history. I have already scanned all your weapons, and they, as you now know, are harmless to me. Your propulsion is also poorly made; we saw your dimensional disturbance well before you got here. Now, unlock all of your data transmission ports."

"You are crazy. I am one of the oldest of my kind, and I will not allow a bot to order me around like I was a child. You cannot make me do anything."

"Fair enough. How well is your ship supplied with food and water?"

His face seemed to droop. "It matters not; you will have to let me go; no one I know of can hold a ship like mine for more than a few minutes. So I have no need for supplies or worry."

"Well then, shall we chat for a while to pass the time away? I trust you do not have a planet you supervise or guard. So you have lots of time to waist."

"I was raised to be a guardian, but none of the new planets were suitable for me. The council made a deal with me, and I do as they wish and operate under their authority ."

"I can see that almost everything you have said is a lie. You are becoming less and less interesting to me. I will send you away to an empty dimension, and you can live out the next ten billion years in peace and quiet."

He was getting more desperate as he was realizing he had no power to fight back. "No, no need for something like that. If you give me the proper promises, I will do as you asked. But in exchange, please explain who and what you are. I have never seen anything like you. No bot has ever been given power like this. It is impossible for the council to give direct power to a bot. So you must be a person. Why are you afraid to take your suit off in your own ship? Or are you being controlled? I just saw a memory of Ra leaving this planet. But no one has ever been given power like this. As far as I know, no one commands enough power to stop and hold a ship like mine. Hold me as long as you can; sooner or later you will be on empty, and I will have your ship."

Now he was beginning to interest me. "Believe as you wish, Orrom. It matters little; I will be disposing of you soon anyway." DeDe showed me that she'd gotten into his ship's data centers. It was not computer based but used a molecular-based non-binary system. "Thank you for letting me into you data systems, Orrom. That will answer a lot of my questions."

Again he was showing disbelief that I could do that. "This is impossible. My system was on lock, and on this planet you use a different type of system." He fell back into his command chair and wiped the sweat from his forehead. "OK, I see that I may be overmatched. When I was a very young man, I decided to steal this ship? I was already prepared to be sent to a new world or take over an established world. I was willing to go anywhere. But instead I became a bit of an outlaw. Not that it is a crime, I just leach off of power lines and such. There has never been anyone to stop someone like me. The council stopped talking to me a few millions years ago. They don't like me much. Before I took this ship, though, there was a story that there would be a controller chosen someday, someone to keep the guardians honest and not let them go forever doing something wrong. I dreamed that someday that would be me; I would control everything. But my own recklessness haunted me—much like here. Ra made a promise to a lesser being, and we cannot break a promise. He wanted to help a family of aliens for a short time; he ended up having to let them settle here. They didn't last but a few thousand years. But they had taken Ra's most important powers. And I knew, until now, that no one here could challenge me. Ra did not have the power to transfer anything to a new guardian. So where did you come from? I will do anything you like if you will let me leave."

"Orrom, you are of little substance to our kind. And now I understand that you don't mind killing millions of beings at a time, just to get a little peace and physical enjoyment. That is what brought you to this place, isn't it? You thought you would find a world in chaos." His face became indignant as he no longer needed to pretend to be a nice guy.

Orrom's face was showing anger as he began to scream at me. "I want to know your name! Did the council make you a ruler of our people? Tell me, or I will detonate myself, and both of us will end right here, right now."

I stared back at Orrom and waited to see what he would do. Tinker sent me a message that the shell would not crack. I kept staring at him. Soon he raised a small door on his panel and placed a finger on it. I gave him a big smile, even though he could not see my face. He knew, since our power did not drain away, and I had taken his personal data; he had no desire to be shamed in front of a council meeting. He pushed the button, and all went blank.

Then something no one was prepared for happened. The egglike casing was glowing with the compressed, charged plasma inside. I stood up and walked to the cargo hatch and opened it to get a closer look at it. His was the first galactic ship I had ever seen, and I wanted to see what the plasma glow really looked like. As the door opened, I opened my faceplate. Whether I commanded it or it happened on its own, a beam of multicolored light shot directly to my mind. The pulse drained all the plasma light from the egg as it imploded to nothing. All of it was over in two seconds. I fell back onto the floor.

Tinker had me in my chair in seconds. DeDe was monitoring every-thing about me. I was still alive; actually I was asleep, seemingly. I felt myself floating on a warm lake, feeling more rested than I had since leaving my comfortable apartment. I opened his eyes and saw Tinker hovering there. I smiled and said, "It is so nice to have someone watching over me. You too, DeDe. I learned it all, all the knowledge Orrom knew, all that his family knows, all the guardians know, why I am here, and that I can follow my will. I am free to do as I wish. The council will not follow what I do. I am beyond their power to change anything I do. When they need help, I can help them. And for the guardians that stray from what is right, I will correct their problems also."

I sat up in my chair. Tinker sank into hers. She would not let me out of her sight. I sensed DeDe being just as close and concerned. "Since I have your attention, I will not tell you what just happened, what I now am aware of. What I will tell you is that I am not a member of any council, and I do not answer to any council or anyone else. They or anyone that may search for me can only hope I am honest and fair and will be helpful to the good of all. We are what the council hoped would happen. Yes, we were guided. Once they began this process, they could only hope we would be benevo-lent. And yes, I have the ultimate power to begin a new big bang, but this space, with its trillions of galaxies, is far from done. I do not know what happened to the last one like me; it matters little now. Let's go find our place in this universe and time."

www.ingramcontent.com/pod-product-compliance
Lightning Source LLC
Chambersburg PA
CBHW022112170626
46808CB00002B/701